"Move Aside, Will You, Irish?"

Max ordered. "Anger isn't good for the baby."

Irish held out her hand. "The key, Max. Then just pack up your stuff, and mosey on down the road. You're not staying."

"The hell I'm not," he said quietly, looking very tough and determined. Not at all a likely daddy candidate. "I intend to be a parent to our baby, Irish. Fight me, and I'll cause hell. There are such things as paternal rights."

"You wouldn't dare, Van Damme—" she began hotly. Before she could move, he tugged her to him, then carefully, possessively, placed his mouth over hers.

The long, sweet kiss left her hungry and limp, melting against him. When his head lifted, his features had softened in the dim light.

"I told you my biological urges hadn't been stirred before I met you," he whispered. "And now you'll have to suffer the consequences for opening the door. At my age, it's not likely that I'll get another chance at parenting, and I intend to enjoy every minute of our pregnancy. I'm putting down roots, sweetheart," he told her. Then he kissed her again.

Dear Reader:

Welcome to Silhouette Desire! If you're a regular reader, you already know you're in for a treat. If this is your first Silhouette Desire, I predict you'll be hooked on romance, because these are sensuous, emotional love stories written by and for today's women—women just like *you!*

A Silhouette Desire can have many different moods and tones: some are humorous, others dramatic. But they *all* have a heroine you can identify with. She's busy, smart, and occasionally downright frazzled! She's always got something keeping her on the go: family, sometimes kids, maybe a job and there's that darned car that keeps breaking down! And of course, she's got that extra complication—the sexy, interesting man she's just met....

Speaking of sexy men, don't miss May's *Man of the Month* title, *Sweet on Jessie,* by Jackie Merritt. This man is just wonderful. Also, look for *Just Say Yes,* another terrific romance from the pen of Dixie Browning. Rounding out May are books by Lass Small, Rita Rainville, Cait London and Christine Rimmer. It's a great lineup, and naturally I hope you read them all.

So, until next month, happy reading!

Lucia Macro
Senior Editor

CAIT LONDON

THE DADDY CANDIDATE

SILHOUETTE *Desire*®

Published by Silhouette Books New York

America's Publisher of Contemporary Romance

SILHOUETTE BOOKS
300 East 42nd St., New York, N.Y. 10017

THE DADDY CANDIDATE

Copyright © 1991 by Lois Kleinsasser-Testerman

ISBN: 0-373-05641-9

First Silhouette Books printing May 1991

All the characters in this book are fictitious. Any
resemblance to actual persons, living or dead, is
purely coincidental.

Printed in the U.S.A.

Books by Cait London

Silhouette Desire

The Loving Season #502
Angel vs. MacLean #593
The Pendragon Virus #611
The Daddy Candidate #641

CAIT LONDON

lives in the Missouri Ozarks but grew up in Washington and still loves craggy mountains and the Pacific coast. She's a full-time secretary, a history buff and an avid reader who knows her way around computers. She grew up painting—landscapes and wildlife—but is now committed to writing and enjoying her three creative daughters. Cait has big plans for her future—learning to fish, taking short trips for research and meeting people. She also writes as Cait Logan and has won *Romantic Times*'s Best New Romance Writer award for 1986.

To Karla Dawn, the amazing one

One

"Maxwell Van Damme. Systems Warrior. I'll bet Madame Abagail LaRue Whitehouse wouldn't invite him into her bordello for a fun time," Irish Dalton muttered, replacing the updated antique telephone in its cradle. Irish forced herself to breathe calmly, inhaling the fresh air flowing in through the open window. She waited for the Colorado breeze, filled with scents of May and pine, to calm her. Not even the aroma of whole-wheat cinnamon rolls wafting from her kitchen could take the edge off her temper.

Tapping her fingers on the windowsill, Irish surveyed her TLC kingdom and thought of Van Damme swooping nearer. She'd been expecting his call, but nothing could have prepared her for the raspy, clipped and arrogant male voice informing her that he would be arriving in one hour and twenty-five minutes.

From the sound of his voice, Irish expected Van Damme to be cut from the same mold as Mark, her ex-fiancé. Unshakable, even at emotional moments, he'd have wires for veins, electronic impulses for heartbeats. A child playing with puppies couldn't warm the steely cockles of his heart. Kittens would scamper to safety in his wake. Wood violets and mountain daisies would wilt as he passed by; bees wouldn't make honey...

Irish frowned, vowing to protect her vacation health spa and inn. Originally a bordello, for years the inn and surrounding ranch land had provided rest and care to those with troubled hearts. A hundred and thirty years ago, Colorado miners knew they could come to Madame Abagail Whitehouse's bordello for understanding and care. Abagail had stepped between her two lovers in a duel, taking the deadly bullets and expiring in her elegant, red velvet boudoir. But somehow Irish doubted that even Abagail's loving heart could cherish a Maxwell Van Damme.

Irish liked to think the madam still inhabited the inn, drifting through the restored rooms in a cloud of lavender scent. One of Irish's TLC theories was that romance was good for the soul, and it was her duty to perpetuate the memory of the madam in a ghostly manner. But with Van Damme on a calculator rampage...Irish shuddered.

"A regular profit-and-loss hit man, and he'll be here for a week, no more than two," Irish repeated Van Damme's estimation through her teeth. "He thinks he can systemize and flatten my TLC business, does he?"

Standing in her large sunlit kitchen, Irish impatiently tapped her sneaker against the restored and varnished boards of her inn.

"My sister is at the bottom of this," Irish accused as she glanced through the window of her bed-and-breakfast health farm. "Katherine 'Angel' MacLean, attorney for the underdog," she muttered over the morning call of the mockingbird sitting on her picket fence. "I've always had the feeling that she wants revenge for my matchmaking—and now it's payback time."

Six years ago Irish had decided that her sister, Katherine, and J.D. MacLean, with whom she'd had a disastrous affair many years earlier, needed each other. Irish had set herself up as bait by allowing J.D. to help her out of a financial bog. Actually a few financial debts hadn't worried Irish, but Katherine had been incensed when J.D. reentered her life via her sister. Their rematch had equaled a shootout, and now the MacLeans had two children: his orphaned grandson, Travis, and a beautiful daughter, four-year-old Dakota. The MacLeans were impressive, tough and invincible when they worked together on a project.

J.D., the lean dark foil to Katherine's blond elegance, was also Irish's business partner. In the five years since he'd married Katherine, J.D. had continued to hold off his wife's instincts to take over her baby sister.

Then two weeks ago, J.D. had called. "The business is too big for your bookkeeping system. The winter ski season is showing as much profit as the summer. You've got repeat guests and an exclusive waiting list."

"So?" she had asked, trusting him. "We've always managed, haven't we? Red-apple cookie jar for big questionable bills, and the shoe box for lesser ones? And now that Jeff is perking things up..."

The name of the inn's manager had hung in the static silence for a moment before J.D. answered. "I think Abagail's is at a crucial turning point. It has exceeded my limits of time. When the bookkeeper untied the knot on the trash bag holding your receipts and bills, she fainted and threatened to sue for mental cruelty. We need an efficiency expert, and I've already called Maxwell Van Damme. Max knows how to cut the flab...."

Flab? Irish had remembered something Katherine had said. "Wait a minute. I remember something about flab, as in Kat's reference to my people." Irish had sighted down on J.D. "You're sending a hit man in here, aren't you?"

"Max or Katherine. Take your choice."

"Some choice. Send in your hit man. Anyone would be better than Katherine when she starts nitpicking."

Now, expecting Van Damme to arrive shortly—in one hour and seventeen minutes—Irish muttered, "Just knowing that...that man is invading my home, jamming his sneaky little nose into my business and messing with my people is enough to turn a chili pepper cold. Nod and smile, that's what I'll do. Then put everything back just the way I like it after he's gone. He's not going to efficientize one single little peony petal," Irish growled, glancing out the window. "I will not use prepared mixes and canned vegetables."

Granny, stooped with age, moved slowly through the field of sweet corn inspecting the green shoots. Granny and her husband, Link, were rest-home runaways who'd arrived at the inn the day after Irish. "We're here to work, missy. Link and I are too young for any old folks home. Besides, it ain't fittin' for a pretty unmarried thing to be here alone," she'd said, eyeing Irish up and down. Then her wrinkles had shifted into a wary smile. "We'll work for our keep. Think we can stay?"

Now the inn was their home. Nadia was the next addition to Irish's family. A recovered alcoholic, unemployed fortune-teller, Nadia's bus fare had run out in Kodiac. The ex-nightclub performer had hated fresh air and people in general. Now Nadia ate an apple and chatted pleasantly with a middle-aged couple debating divorce. Beneath the shade of the maple tree, she plucked coins from behind ears and pried smiles from their tense faces. Nadia knew what soothed aching hearts, and she applied her fortunes like a sweet healing balm.

Irish firmed her lips, wondering if hit men smiled. "Van Damme," she muttered, inspecting the new erosion cutting down the ski slope. Looking over the newly plowed fields and the rows of sprouting plants, she mumbled, "Sounds like a Great Dane. He probably never heard of eating alfalfa sprouts or hugging. A workaholic numbers person who thinks profit is more important than caring.''

The calculator-for-a-heart image slid into another man's face, and thinking of Mark, Irish sighed and closed her eyes, ignoring the chug-rattle rhythm of the new water heater that threatened to expire with its warranty.

Seven and a half years ago she'd walked out on a five-year relationship with Mark. Looking back, their stark personality differences stood out like granite tombstones. Her degree in home economics hadn't prepared her for the office position that he had insisted she accept. While Irish had filed and typed and dreamed of a home packed with children, Mark had been perfectly happy. But when he had ordered Irish to have a sterility operation, she took one long gasp and decided she'd opt for a house filled with children. Then she'd packed her favorite cookware, her pots of herbs, and walked out.

Irish had bequeathed Mark her exercise mat and videotapes for trimming hips. He'd have to find someone else to be his willowy delight. Whatever lay ahead for her, it wasn't a nightly battle to keep the inches off her rounded posterior.

Wrapping the shreds of her heart in her forgotten home-economics degree, Irish had marched off to find her special niche.

She'd fallen in love with Abagail's house from the moment she'd first seen it. Deserted, staring at her with broken windows, the inn shimmered in the dry Colorado sun. Graffiti had been scrawled across the siding's peeling paint, and the orange neon hotel sign swung in a creaky tune.

Plopping her tiny savings and an amount from a bank loan down in front of the owner, Irish had purchased Abagail's. Now the restored rooms were filled with antique ornate furniture, and Abagail's Inn rated stars across the health-spa catalogs. Since she'd bought the former bordello, she'd shored up sagging hearts with large doses of TLC. Restored by her care and healthy food, her recycled, revamped and happy people returned to their individual worlds.

Unable to hold her dark mood, Irish smiled at the sight of a husband and wife, both stressed-out executives, kissing and whispering like teenagers in love for the first time. The couple sat on a wooden bench, holding hands and snuggling.

She grinned impishly as a young couple kissed in the shadows of a weeping willow. Later in the season, the inn would be filled with couples recapturing their love. When the Romaines had stopped at the inn to ask for directions, Mrs. Romaine mentioned that they needed time away from their three small children but couldn't afford the lovely spa's fee. Lacy and Nigel, now wrapped in each other's arms, had been ecstatic to discover they were the winners of Irish's new one hundredth customer-free-vacation prize.

Wrapping her arms around herself, Irish gave herself a hug. People needed hugs, she thought, tucking Maxwell Van Damme into a ''later'' pocket with the lawn mower that had died.

Maxwell Van Damme glanced in his rearview mirror, then shifted into a higher gear to pass the pickup truck. On the winding uphill curve, he allowed himself to enjoy the sleek sensuous power of the Porsche gliding over the Colorado Rocky pass. He shifted again, easing the engine for a smooth stretch of highway. On either side of the road, the one-o'clock sun tangled in the vivid sweeps of May foliage. Shadows hovered in the ravines, melding blues and purples with browns and ochres.

Running his palm around the steering wheel, Max savored the responsive powerful engine. Stretching in the low custom seat, he eased the drive from Lake Tahoe from the cramped muscles of his six-foot body. He appreciated good machinery and neat business systems tuned to perfection. Max's life-style reflected the same streamlining, free of attachments and clutter.

A doe and her fawn watched the car from the protection of a sumac stand, and Max smiled. Protective of her fawn, the doe reminded him of Katherine MacLean's description of her sister. "By nature, Irish is so loving, she doesn't see that the people she's collected at her bed-and-breakfast are using her. At thirty-three, she hasn't got a selfish bone in her body."

Glancing at a passing road sign, Max slipped a Bach cassette into the Porsche's sophisticated sound system. The town of Kodiac and Abagail's Inn, his destination, lay twenty-two minutes away. Settling comfortably into the customized seat, Max allowed the classical music to pour into him.

He liked fine music, good wine and gourmet foods, and had planned to enjoy all three after streamlining the sales and reservation systems of a popular resort chain in Tahoe. He'd discovered the perfect rental condominium, stocked with all the copper pots and chef's knives an experienced cook could want. Max had relished diving into his favorite recipes, cooking his favorite gourmet dishes.

But J.D. had requested a favor, and Max had agreed. He smiled quickly, the movement not reaching his eyes behind the mirrorlike sunglasses. J.D. was the closest thing to a friend and family that Max had ever had. The senseless brawl was years ago, but Max remembered vividly how J.D. had fought with him, back to back, against eight angry men.

Max slashed a glance at an elaborately scrolled sign that read: "Abagail's Inn. Health Spa and Inn. Let us take care of you. Tender Loving Care is our middle name."

He shifted briskly, rounding a curve shaded by stately firs. At forty-two, he'd long ago learned that love wasn't designed to mesh with his personal systems.

Max switched his thoughts to the task waiting for him. Apparently, Irish Dalton, a natural earth-mother personality, ran her inn with all the business aplomb of a child sucking her thumb and picking tulips. Concerned about her, J.D. and Katherine had asked Max to structure a fail-safe business system for the inn. The MacLeans had agreed that it wouldn't be easy. Irish had different ideas about the people she had tucked beneath her protective wing.

He took a deep breath, absorbing the mellow music as he thought of Irish Dalton, J.D.'s partner and owner of the health spa and inn. Sorting what he knew about the situation into neat labeled mental boxes, Max remembered Irish's lilting happy tones when she'd answered the telephone. Those welcome tones had changed abruptly once he informed her that he was Max Van Damme.

"I know who and what you are, Max," she had said tightly. "You're expected. You're welcome to stay and rest here. You're even welcome to snoop around. We only have a few guests so I suppose you can't do much damage. But you will not—I repeat, not—even suggest to any of my people the reason for your visit here. If you do, you're out on your ear," she had finished lightly before the line went dead.

Max slowed the car at Kodiac's city limits, quickly noting the typical Western setting, described by J.D. as "a wide spot in the road." He noted the gas station, the customary truck-stop café and grocery store, and a few houses surrounded by large gardens and picket fences. He slowed the Porsche even more as a child rode a horse across the road, followed by two smaller children, who watched him warily.

Glancing at the rugged soaring mountains cradling the valley, Max hoped the inn was quiet and childfree.

A butterfly drifted across a flower bed, reminding Max of Dakota, who never stayed long in one place. Unaccustomed to children, Max had found himself anticipating her swift, moist lollypop-flavored kisses. The MacLean children reflected their parents' love and gave hugs and kisses unreservedly. At first Max had been uncomfortable, but now he looked forward to visiting the MacLean household.

Though he enjoyed J.D.'s children, Max didn't fit into the parent mold. The Van Damme genes didn't contain a loving nature. He hadn't seen his parents for years. Elena and Franz Van Damme, genetic scientists, hadn't missed their son from the moment he was born.

He smiled again tightly as he remembered himself at nineteen, responding hotly in the experienced hands of an older woman. After a series of teenage encounters, he'd been ripe for the situation. Starved for affection and deceived by his hormones, Max thought he'd found love; but Natalie was merely between husbands, and young Max didn't qualify.

On the rebound and out to soothe his damaged masculinity, Max had married Jennifer, a stockbroker. For seven years, she had been supportive of his studies and his budding career. His needs had appeared to be hers, and neither one of them had wanted children. She had been the young executive's perfect wife and partner. Max had thought the marriage would last forever.

But Jennifer's needs had been greater, and when he'd returned home unexpectedly one night, Max found his wife wrapped in the arms of her lover, his best friend. In the scene that had followed, Neil had suffered a broken collarbone and two cracked ribs. Max had been stunned by the emotions spewing from him—he hadn't liked them. He'd spent a year getting over the pain, trying to block out the scene and pasting himself back together.

Rounding a curve, Max spotted the rambling bed-and-breakfast, circled by a white picket fence that badly needed painting. The blurred image of Jennifer and Neil, wrapped in damp sheets, clicked off as Max surveyed Irish's property.

The hundred acres of fields and ski slopes sprawled around Abagail's, enfolding it like a dollhouse set on a colorful patchwork blanket. The house seemed to twist at odd angles, blending old cornices and wide porches and high pointed roofs with newer practical additions. Absently noting the rocking chairs lined across the front porch, and the elderly couple occupying two of them, Max parked his car by the front gate.

Through the Porsche's window, he noted a man dressed in work clothes leaning against the trunk of a maple tree. The man glanced at Max, then continued to watch a woman kneeling on a spot in a freshly plowed garden. In her wake, tiny green shoots formed an uneven line. When the man said something and eyed Max, the woman stood up. She dusted her hands on her dirty jeans and looked at Max. Framed by green fields, the young woman fitted Katherine's description of Irish.

Irish said something to the man, then carefully picked her way over the maze of zigzagging garden rows toward Max. In midstride she hesitated, glanced down at a new plant bed and bent to tend it.

Max placed his glasses inside his dress shirt pocket. She wasn't happy; she looked like a mother tiger stalking a predator who had come too near her cub. Irish didn't look particularly good-natured, nor susceptible to leaners-on.

She looked very hot and very passionate.

The thought startled Max, tightening his taut stomach. These days, wrapped in the comfort of his experience and age, he rarely thought of women as hot and passionate, nor soft and sweet. She reminded him of Tchaikovsky's passionate strains, rather than Bach's smoothly integrated chords. Max stirred against the leather seat restlessly, uncomfortable with his comparison of Irish to his favorite composers.

But as she walked toward the front gate, the late afternoon sun caught reddish sparks from her short curly blond hair. Max had a quick image of animation and light, sunlight and smiles, all at the same time. Her T-shirt and jeans had seen better times, though Max reluctantly admired her soft curves.

His gaze returned to her face. Irish had an all-American face with wide blue eyes and a strong jaw. Her pert nose

suited her freckles, and a soft vulnerable mouth caused
Max to think of California strawberries—not the large, too-
sweet variety, but the medium size with the interesting tart
flavor.

He glanced uneasily away from her T-shirt as she hopped
over the row of peonies lining the brick walkway to the
house. She moved like an athlete, the inn's TLC logo flowing over her quivering breasts. Distracted momentarily,
Max thought they were nice breasts. Not too full, nor too
slight.

His hands tightened on the steering wheel. In his palms,
they would feel exactly right. About the size of succulent
Valencia oranges, though the tips probably would have the
slight nuance and mellow bite of a fine French wine.

Startled momentarily by the turn of his thoughts as he
compared Irish Dalton to a gourmet's delight, Max swallowed to moisten his unaccountably dry throat. There were
always reasons behind his emotions, and he suddenly remembered he hadn't been sexually active for quite some
time. Irish Dalton, walking barefoot through the early-
afternoon sun with the sprawling ancient house behind her,
caused him to be uneasy. Max almost discarded the
thought, but then Irish lifted her hand to brush away an
errant reddish-gold curl. The movement brought her short
T-shirt higher, revealing a smoothly indented waist that
emphasized her rounded hips.

They would be soft hips, cushiony hips with the bones
moving smoothly beneath the surface. A man could settle
within her deeply and bask in the undulating warmth . . .

Max frowned, sliding out of the low-slung car to stand
his full height. He shifted restlessly, stretching cramped
muscles. Tuned to the needs of his lean body, Max per-
ceived a definite sexual tension running through it. The
thought made him uncomfortable, like systems with funny
little imbalances. Since Jennifer, Max had exerted perfect
control over his emotions and his body.

He pressed his lips together grimly. Evidently fatigue and truck-stop food had taken their toll on him.

Irish Dalton had that round soft look that his parents had classified as good potential childbearing material. And then Max tucked a third, nonlogical thought into his mental-Irish box: he wondered, with quick intense emotion, if Irish Dalton had a lover to kiss the freckles dancing across her nose. And taste the sunlight caught on the silvery tips of her reddish-blond eyelashes.

The man who had been lounging in the shade sauntered off, and the movement brought Max back to his purpose. He rubbed the taut muscle at the back of his neck, uncomfortable with the knowledge that he'd been distracted by sunlight on a woman's eyelashes.

With customary discipline, Max forced his attention back to the inn.

As she watched J.D.'s hit man survey his intended victim—her beloved inn—Irish firmed her lips.

Van Damme will not touch, systemize, nor dispossess any of my people. He will not change one hardwood floorboard, nor gossamer rose curtain. If he inoculates Abagail's with electronic room service, I'll rip out the whats-its. I'll...

Irish smiled tightly and glanced at his immaculately polished car, nesting under her shade tree. If Van Damme parked under that tree for an evening, he'd have a polkadot, bird-decorated car.

"Get ready, Madame," she whispered to the resident ghost as she moved toward Van Damme, the systems warrior. "You and I have a mission. There's a carpetbagger approaching at high noon."

The black Porsche well represented the man, Maxwell Van Damme. The Black Knight on a mission. He looked sleek, and honed to suit his purpose. An efficiency expert with dark thick brows and a hard unsmiling mouth. As he moved around the car to meet her, she resented his height, resented his presence and the hard I'm-taking-charge way he walked toward her.

She gripped the mud ball in her hand more tightly. Van Damme's purpose was to mess with her land, and she intended to give him the feel of it immediately.

He looked exactly like what he was—a businessman, cutting the warmth and affection from his life by hurrying through all the whimsies that make life enjoyable and make people lovable, Irish thought sadly. She noted the hard well-shaved face, the slashing dark brown eyes that estimated and dissected everything in their sweep. His skin lacked laughter lines, and a taut muscle moved in his jaw as though he couldn't wait to accomplish his mission and soar out of the wilderness in his shiny car.

Irish glanced at his car. He probably loved it as much as she loved her inn. After all, hit men/systems warriors deserved their special loves, too.

She sensed that Maxwell Van Damme had never known real love.

She doubted that his auburn hair had ever been mussed by the wind, that its tendency to curl had ever been freed; she doubted he laughed easily or exclaimed with delight.

She wondered who and what would make him smile, lighting his cold dark eyes with warmth.

"Hello, Max," she said quietly, returning his stony unreadable gaze evenly. "Are you hungry?"

He flicked a wary look down his nose at her, as though she were a wrinkle that needed ironing. Though Max probably never experienced a wrinkle or a gravy stain in his life, he needed attention, just like a little lost boy, she thought whimsically. She allowed her lips to curve with the thought.

Instinctively, Irish placed her clean hand on his forearm and felt the ridges of muscle contract beneath the warm hairy surface. He withdrew fractionally from her light touch, and then she knew with certainty that Maxwell Van

Damme was hers to take care of—even if he was on a devastation mission.

"I'm fine, thank you," he returned with a curt dip of his head. Irish noted the deep rough texture of his voice. Max hesitated slightly, then formally extended his hand. Max was a cautious man, moving through life by picking each step carefully, she decided, and smiled gently up at him.

But he'd stepped onto the lily pads of her precious pond, and Mr. Van Damme was on his own.

When Irish stepped closer, she caught the masculine scents of expensive after-shave and soap. And when his hand wrapped around her smaller one, flattening the mud on it, she felt safety in his touch. He released her hand immediately, and Irish stepped back, wriggling her toes in the sun-warmed grass and clasping her hands behind her innocently. Van Damme's hand was large; the broad palm had aligned neatly with hers, his fingers strong as they'd curled around her hand. She had the impression of controlled power, self-confidence and efficiency all at the same time. Of course there was disdain, too, as if his hand had never touched mud.

Impishly Irish wondered if Van Damme ever let his control slip. Would he take a second piece of her special deep-dish Dutch apple pie?

She glanced at his flat stomach and decided Van Damme never exceeded the proper limits of anything.

He looked down at his palm and frowned slightly, then extracted a carefully folded monogrammed handkerchief from his pocket. She felt a guilty twinge about her mud-ball revenge. "I hope you enjoy your stay, Max. I'll show you to your room so you can rest before dinner. We're having apple pie for dessert, and one of the guests is churning the ice cream now. The recipe uses fresh cow's milk and brown farm eggs. If you have any dietary restrictions, please let me know," she said, watching his quick assessing glances dart over her beloved inn as he wiped his hand dry.

"That would be fine," he said in that get-away-from-me tone, noticing the lawn mower that Jeff had left in pieces two days ago.

While Max thought he was setting up an efficiency system for her, she would be giving him the warmth he so badly needed. Plants, animals, humans and Travis Mac-Lean's guppies had responded to her. Max would, too. She'd put him back in his shiny sleek car with a warm feeling, and her TLC business would continue on its original loving course.

"Laundry service is free," she said, taking the handkerchief from him. "I hope you like health food."

As Max swung his leather bag from the Porsche, Irish continued. "It's our specialty here at Abagail's Inn. Although it's mostly just-like-mom-used-to cooking."

Irish winked, impishly testing Max's formality. "Let me know how your mother prepared your favorite dish, and I'll give it a try."

"Whatever is on the menu will be fine." Max rounded the car and slashed her a grim look, then glanced suspiciously up at the rustling in the tree boughs. He had just the right stay-away-from-me look to intrigue Irish. The look made her want to stroke his darkly tanned brow, pet his tense neck and ease his . . .

Irish swallowed, caught by the sunlit patch of hair exposed by his opened collar.

As Max turned to survey Abagail's and the surrounding fields in the dusky light, Irish was presented with a full magnificent view of Van Damme's elegant backside.

From broad shoulders to trim waist and taut buttocks, Maxwell Van Dame seemed . . . touchable. She pondered the thought, flicking a curious and, she admitted, a slightly naughty glance down the length of his long legs clad in dress slacks. She knew without a doubt that the first free moment he had, Max would polish the Colorado dust from his Italian loafers.

Despite Max's occupation, his body seemed very hard and fit, she decided analytically. Not that she was really interested in him as a, well, male person. Good heavens, she'd had enough problems after the breakup with Mark.

Irish shrugged mentally, thinking of the wide variety of men who occasionally foraged through her affections. She liked a dinner date or a movie now and then, sprinkled with light hand-holding and a fond good-night kiss. She liked the scent of after-shave and a hot round of dancing to rock and roll.

Max looked more like the tango-type: smooth, stylish, unruffled, and structured down to his Italian loafers. Yet something pulsed beneath the surface, maybe a fiery flamenco with riveting guitars and castanets.

Max rolled a shoulder to ease his muscles, drawing the expensive wrinkle-free fabric tightly across the hard contour. Irish's fingers twitched just once with the urge to stroke it.

Mimi, a tiger-colored barn cat and a mother several times over, loped from the porch to Max. She stopped and leaned against him. Weaving happily around his legs, the feline hussy rubbed and purred as though she'd found her heart's delight.

Max shot Mimi his get-away-from-me look, and the cat grinned hopefully up at him, twitching her tail. Max nudged her away slightly, and Mimi leaned against him in a rhapsody of purring and rubbing.

Irish enjoyed the scene of a wrinkle-free perfect hit man waylaid by a cat. Max hesitated, bent stiffly and unerringly scratched the spot behind the cat's ear. Mimi pressed against his hand for a minute and licked it fondly. Then she lifted her tail high and sauntered away from him like a lover after a satisfying romp.

"Mimi's friendly," Irish offered, amused as Max's gaze warily tracked the cat into the snowball bushes. Actually Mimi never lowered herself to brazen seduction, preferring to let the guests seek her ears and tummy without invitation.

"Come along then, Max. I've prepared a lovely room for you," she said lightly and watched with pleasure as his head went back as though he'd taken a slap. Max wasn't accustomed to being patronized, nor to taking orders. She'd have to remember that if he tried to flatten her TLC policies with profit-and-loss statements.

Irish turned and began walking up the brick path to the inn, leaving him to follow. She waved to a passing neighbor child and fought a smile. Maxwell Van Damme would keep his hands off her business, and he would enjoy his stay, she promised herself. J.D. and Katherine had sent her someone to care for, because if ever a person needed her care, it was Max.

Max walked behind Irish, drawn to the buoyant confident stride and the intriguing softness of her hips. Instinctively Max calculated the amount of sway to a fraction of an inch. He reluctantly enjoyed the feminine flow for an instant as though it were the strains of Bach. A familiar scent followed in her wake, of cinnamon and freshly baked bread, and an elusive, enticing scent of warm womanly skin lying on cool sun-dried sheets.

Startled by the flow of his thoughts, he forced his gaze upward, noting the indentation of her waist and the soft curve of her shoulders.

The late-afternoon sun caught and played in her riotous curls, and he had the impression of gold dust on dewy strawberries. As she'd stood beneath the sunlight and maple-tree shadows, Irish Dalton had caused Max's body to harden sensually.

He frowned, remembering Katherine's description of her sister—*Irish is magic; she gets inside people and makes them feel good.*

His frown deepened; no one had really gotten inside or to him since his childhood. He could almost feel her wrap around him, the softness and the warmth.

Why did he want to place his mouth on her soft one and take all she could give?

Why did he want her softness enveloping him, keeping him warm and soothing the tense years away?

Dammit! Why was his body hard, honed intensely to the moving softness of Irish's?

For just that fraction of a second, Max needed what she could give....

Then Irish paused, looking at him over her shoulder, her soft lips parted to say something. Her blue eyes were warm with laughter, and Max fell straight into them.

Their gazes held momentarily, then Irish's widened. Max stepped closer, wanting to inhale the meadow-flower scent, wanting...

He could feel his passion snake through him, leaving heat in its wake. He hadn't felt stark desire for years, and now it tugged sharply at his lower stomach, the intensity painful and unyielding.

Beneath his shadow, Irish's face paled. Her eyes flickered slightly and darkened to cobalt blue. Max knew Irish felt the intensity, the smashing heat driving him.

The tip of her tongue flicked moisture onto her bottom lip, and the wild surge of desire riveted Max beneath the sunlight and shadows, intertwining him with a woman he very much wanted to explore. He wanted to lay her down on the lush spring clover and grass....

In that instant, he knew her skin would be dewy fresh, soft as rose petals. She'd taste like sweet mountain air and exotic sensual mists. In that same instant, he knew he wanted her as he'd never wanted another woman.

She shivered despite the warm day, easing away from him.

Head back, the sunlight twisting through her hair, her cheeks flushed, Irish shot him a look of queenly distaste. "No, Max," she said quietly, turning away.

Two

Seated at the family-style dinner table that night, Max dutifully answered the questions he was asked. In his experience with groups, especially those of the relating and happy type, curiosity about him lasted until dessert. Then he could distance himself from the necessary chatter and begin sifting through the guests and staff. And in this instance, a cowboy who showed signs of territorial rights around Irish topped the list.

Max allowed himself to enjoy freshly baked whole-wheat bread and a rice-and-broccoli-and-chicken dish with delicate seasonings. The plain, tasty and healthy cuisine suited the country atmosphere.

He glanced at the whimsical garden salad. The chunks of crisp greens had obviously been savaged by a mad strangler. Reluctantly Max approved of the herbs drifting in the various fresh salad dressings. Except the vinaigrette dressing, which lacked Dijon mustard.

Max forced himself away from the tempting dissection of Irish's freestyle cookery. And the fact, of course, that he hadn't noted one copper pot, nor chef's knife in the kitchen. In a San Francisco gourmet shop, he'd spotted a beautiful knife, with a wide blade just right for smashing garlic cloves—but he'd always traveled lightly, unable to collect gleaming copper pots and a proper selection of knives. The antique oak chopping table in the sunny kitchen was magnificent....

Max frowned, realizing that the friendly atmosphere and savory aromas had momentarily seduced him. Setting himself back on track, Max sorted his thoughts, avoiding the mental controversy of Dijon mustard.

Max pushed the sliver of Dutch apple pie through the creamy ice cream, savoring the delicate sweet-and-tart taste of the fruit. Baked in a quiche dish in lieu of a proper pan hadn't changed the flavor. An apple chunk reminded him of the cookie jar and the shoe box he'd found placed on the bed in his room.

Stuffed with receipts, the shoe box, which contained Irish's notorious bookkeeping system, created an instant headache for Max. Irish kept scraps of paper that had obviously been through a washing machine. The blurred totals on the receipts were like something from *The Twilight Zone*. Irish's rounded script, listing denture polish and Dr. Seuss books, appeared on the tax assessor's statement. An outrageous tractor-repair bill, spattered with a raspberry stain, lacked a breakdown of labor and parts. Ditto marks covered the guest register, which was stuffed with pressed dried mountain flowers and assorted food-stained recipes.

Several unopened and outdated notices from major companies proved that she'd accepted credit cards as blithely as freshly baked sugar cookies. Various lists scrolled down the envelopes, one of which read: "Leta Jones cat—three whites, four calico. Order Dutch tulip bulbs. Bake chocolate cake for school supper. Bake cookies for Beth's seventh-grade class."

Concealing his mental shudder, Max allowed the dinner conversation to flow around him as he settled into his thoughts. Irish had also thrust a huge box of letters at him, her eyes dancing with mischief. The letters, as frazzled and spattered with cooking stains as the bills, swelled with gratitude. Max had thrown these thank-yous into the category of paving the way for further nonpaid visits.

He'd glanced at the papers, then decided to walk around the immediate grounds before tackling the project with the help of classical violins and oboes. Mimi had attached herself to him the minute he opened the back door. With the cat on his heels, rubbing and purring against him when he paused, Max had taken a cursory tour of Abagail's.

At first the ranch manager had been friendly, tossing off quick and indefinite answers to Max's questions. Then, when forced to answer specific points, Jeff had clamped his mouth shut and walked off into the fescue fields. After taking notes, Max had returned to the inn.

He cut through the second piece of pie Irish placed in front of him. It was delicious pie with a flaky crust; he found himself enjoying the lattice crust sprinkled with sugar.

Twenty-three people appeared to be just where they wanted to be—seated around the immense cherrywood table, which was draped with a lacy cloth. Irish treated each person with a touch, a smile and a personal comment. Without the bonds of blood, she had formed a family.

Feeling chilled despite the comfortable temperature, Max finished his pie. Throughout dinner, Max had followed the relationships and had cut the paying guests aside, leaving what Irish referred to as her "people." He had them pegged now—persons without financial means. He doubted that the elderly couple, Granny and Link, who helped several of the guests serve food, really justified the good wages, bed and board that Irish paid them.

Beside him, Nadia's bangle bracelets jingled. Nadia was fiftyish, plump, wearing a loose Gypsy blouse and skirt, a shawl and a head scarf, and she didn't like him. She fingered her ornate rings and the tarot cards evident in her pocket and stared ominously at him. Nadia had been laying out her cards constantly since he'd arrived. She had invited him to a tarot session, and Max mentally tucked the offer away. Max guessed that her purpose at the inn—if she had one—was to provide background for the madam's ghost.

Recently Nadia had undergone an operation, and Irish had paid the bill. She'd also paid for Link's hearing aid.

Max sipped the excellent freshly ground house coffee slowly, replacing his cup on the rose china saucer carefully. He glanced at Jeff, who, besides being the ranch manager, was the general repairman. Jeff's signature had been on the repair bills and questionable machinery purchases. Max had jotted down figures for payment of such things as workmen's wages, garage bills and a variety of contract work.

Irish wrote checks for the bills, which she indicated by drawing a smiling face on the receipts. Remembering the checkbook, from a joint account with J.D., Max shivered mentally. He preferred dates, check numbers, payee and amount, to *Flowers. John. School drawing. Tube of cerulean blue for Jonathan.*

Jonathan, the inn's artist, shook aside a wedge of long spiky hair to stare at Max. Jonathan's canvasses, stacked in a side parlor were good, capturing the Rockies with the softness of a Renoir. By wedging himself beneath Irish's protection, Jonathan didn't have to keep himself groomed, pleasant, nor did he have to worry about sales. In Max's opinion, Irish's cushiony nest did nothing but hinder what could be a soaring career.

As Irish poured more coffee into Max's cup, Boonie Riggs shot him a dark look. Apparently this cowboy type frequently placed his dusty boots beneath Irish's well-laden dinner table. Max returned the stare coolly as Irish moved around the table to refill Boonie's cup. Around the toothpick lodged at the side of his mouth, Boonie leered up at Irish. "You're looking pert tonight, honey. Just right for a ride in old Boonie's pickup. Want to go over to my place and watch some television? We'd be alone," he added in a lower suggestive tone that raised the hair on the back of Max's neck.

When Boonie's hand slid around Irish's waist possessively, Max thought fleetingly about placing a painful karate chop on Boonie's wrist. Instead he ran his thumb along the tablecloth, steadily mashing a whole-wheat bread crumb into the lace.

The other guests missed Boonie's low insinuation, but Max did not. Irish smiled softly and bent to whisper, "Don't come here after you've been drinking, Boonie. I know you've had a bad time lately, but you'll just have to manage better—"

"Hell, I could if you'd just spend some time making up with me. Is that dude over there—" he nodded at Max "—the reason you're avoiding me?"

Max glanced at Boonie's jaw and decided the cowboy would understand a fist better than karate. The thought of Irish's soft body nestled against the rancher's made his body tense. Trying to distance himself from such unsettling and unfamiliar emotions, Max stared out the window to the Hereford cattle grazing peacefully in the fields. He rummaged mentally for the soothing strains of Bach—

"Would you like to walk after dinner, Max? You've already walked over the grounds, but I'd love to show you our TLC center. It's so much fun sharing the farm with a first-time guest," Irish invited softly beside him, startling him with those wide vulnerable blue eyes.

For an instant, Max had an image of a clear snow lake in the high mountain country, then he caught a hot menacing look from Boonie. He returned the stare evenly for a moment, allowed a corner of his mouth to rise mockingly. Boonie's scowl darkened, and Max accepted the blatant male challenge with a nod. It pleased him to give the cowboy the wrong impression.

Irish's blue eyes lit up, and she patted his shoulder. Beneath the light touch, Max tensed. *No adult had ever touched him lightly or affectionately.*

"You've been a good boy, Max," she whispered into his ear. "I'm so glad you recognized Jonathan's sensitivity. Not a soul here knows your real mission. Except maybe Nadia, who is a supreme fortune-teller," she added, kissing his taut cheek. "Thank you. Just for that, you can churn our next ice cream."

Placing his silverware exactly one centimeter apart, Max fought the urge to place his hand over his cheek to trap the kiss.

Dusk settled over Abagail's with the nuance of a delicate lace doily. The mountain chill slid down into the valley, bringing with it night sounds and the heavy scents of freshly tilled earth and pine trees. In the distance dogs barked, and cows called to their calves.

As Max walked beside Irish, his dark brown eyes slashed the grounds and swept up the erosion on the ski slope. As he took in the broken white board fence surrounding the cows, Max's expression was unreadable. Irish decided he was calculating losses in big dollar signs.

Then he reached out to pat Morticia the mule. The momentary gesture was more of a brisk tap than a stroke, as if Max wasn't used to giving any part of himself away. When Morticia lifted her head, Max reached out to scratch her ears. Morticia blinked her long lashes at him flirtatiously, lifting her nose for a brief pat. Of course Max was forced to oblige; Irish had noted that Max was very well mannered, if distant. She wondered briefly what Max's grim face would look like sheathed in a genuine smile. She toyed with the idea of his tickle spots and remembered her fleeting but sharp response to his hard body earlier.

She forced herself to stop thinking of Max's hairy chest, his lean stomach and the taut curve of his buns beneath the dress slacks. She preferred to skip through certain sensitive areas in her life, and sensuality was smack in the middle of the briars. His tickle spots were not her concern.

But it wouldn't hurt him to smile, she thought rebelliously as Max glanced around the barn and said, "Needs a new roof and the clutter picked up." He nodded at a dust-covered saddle riding an unpainted fence. "Don't you have a tack room?"

"Why Max, I didn't know you were an authority on barns." Irish teased, wanting to dislodge his grim expression. Max didn't the smile. Irish really didn't like the little quiver of anger that went scratching through her when she smiled again, an expression he met with a cool look down his nose.

Morticia nudged him, begging for another pat, which lingered into an ear-scratching session. Max obviously was an obliging gentleman when it came to mules.

Max had a nice face, Irish decided when they walked through the peony gardens to the herbal ones. His jaw was tense and darkening, promising an evening beard. Irish looked away. Her fingers had just flexed with the need to stroke the taut cord running downward from his jaw to his throat.

She glanced uneasily at the wedge of hair at the base of his throat. It reminded her of Mark's chest.

She felt herself tighten, forcing away the memories of her one affair. In their modern glass-and-chrome apartment, Mark had scheduled lovemaking in the systematic manner he prepared his reports. She plucked a stalk of fescue grass and ripped the head away, tossing the seeds into the evening breeze.

No one could accuse her of not trying to fall in love. She'd dated and tried a variety of kisses. She enjoyed dancing close and feeling feminine; it was just that the special click she wanted hadn't clicked yet.

"The outbuildings are in need of repair, Irish," Max stated in an adult-to-child tone. "J.D. was right to be concerned about his investment here. By the way, I can't find receipts for additional billing charges—room service or the items a guest might require. Where are they?"

"There aren't any. People come here to rest, not deal with business. I try to provide everything they might want, and they have only to ask."

Irish's steamy temper returned when she remembered his reason for visiting Abagail's. "I'm sure you'll rake and gnaw until you get to the bones, won't you, Max? I suppose your real name is the Cruncher?" she asked sharply, surprised at her unusual flare of temper with a man she had just met. "You'll take all the beauty out of TLC and push everything into computers or whatevers. You think in numbers, not in care and love."

A dark brow lifted arrogantly as Max quietly looked down at her. "Do I? How interesting. In what terms does Mr. Riggs think? Or does Mr. Riggs indulge in the process of thinking at all?" he amended coolly, widening his stance as if he'd wait forever to hear an explanation he didn't deserve.

Irish held his stare for a moment and decided that humor couldn't possibly be glinting in the dark depths of his eyes. She bent, plucking a stalk of purple wildflowers and bringing them to her nose. "Be careful, Max," she warned quietly, watching the Romaines stroll off into a stand of isolated pine trees. Nigel Romaine had tucked a blanket beneath his arm. "I could fire you. I'm an equal partner."

Irish rarely argued, and she didn't like the feeling that she was about to jump into one. She could see that her threat hadn't frightened him; his long legs weren't exactly shivering in their locked stance.

His hard mouth moved into a mocking half smile, as if he wanted an out-and-out argument. "Your ranch manager should be fired," Max continued evenly, the gleam in his eyes deepening. He reached down and scratched Mimi's ears. "I'll start computing his figures tonight and will have a report ready for you in the morning. Tomorrow I'll order a computer unit that even a child could understand. *You* might even be able to manage it."

While Irish dealt with her rising anger, Max nodded toward the Romaines. "I doubt they can afford the fee here. There was another couple and the older woman with arthritis—"

"The Smythes and Edith Milway," Irish said between her teeth, glaring up at him. "They received giveaway vacations—you know, for advertising purposes. I've done well here, Max. The inn is always full, except in the worst weather when people don't feel safe making the trip—"

"Charity doesn't equal profits," Max stated in his cool clipped tones. Irish ignored the flickering lights in his eyes. "By the way, do you have qualifications for running this bed-and-breakfast?"

Curling her fingers into her palms, Irish narrowed her eyes at him. "It's a health-care farm, Max—carrot juice, sprouts and lots of smiles, hugs and kisses. We offer humanity, not charity. And I have a degree in home economics," she managed to answer, considering walking back through the cow pasture. Watching Max squish his Italian loafers through fresh cow patties might ease her need for revenge.

Irish didn't like the angry emotions Max could ignite within her. "Do you have a problem with that?"

Max shifted on his legs, crossed his arms and stood regarding her with unnerving patience. "Evidently you opted to skip the accounting classes. Can you use a basic adding machine?"

Irish had the impression that Max was baiting her as punishment for a crime.

"By the way, a vet should be called for your stock," Max added in the same cool tone. "Morticia has dental problems, and several horses could use reshoeing. Their grain isn't quality, and the water trough needs a thorough cleaning."

"Jeff's men take care of those things..." Irish began hotly, then watched Max's arrogant eyebrow lift slowly. "They don't?"

When his other eyebrow lifted, she took a deep breath and said, "I'll look into the matter."

"See that you do. Neglect is animal cruelty, too. I can't abide poor upkeep," Max stated as he neatly sidestepped a cow patty on his way to the tractor parked near the barn lot.

Irish followed, casting a sympathetic look back at Morticia. In two minutes Max had insinuated she wasn't fit to run her business and had thrown in an animal-cruelty charge. Now he was meticulously picking through the entrails of the inn's tractor like a surgeon on his way to a ruptured gall bladder.

He thrust a black oil dipstick beneath her nose as though it were a murderer's bloody blade. "This oil is old. It's starting to turn solid. Upkeep makes equipment last longer, Irish," he added, replacing the dipstick. "I'll want the maintenance schedule for every piece of machinery."

Irish blinked, ignoring his tiny but pleased smirk. "Schedules?"

"For your new computer system," he said slowly, carefully, with a movement around his lips that served as a smug smile. "I'll have you up and running in an efficient system in no time."

Perched on her high four-poster bed, Irish flipped through a magazine and muttered, "Data banks... systems... computers...."

Normally at eleven o'clock she'd be asleep, but Van Damme had intruded into her happy TLC kingdom, slashing his calculator sword through the magic. She took a deep breath, adjusted the twisted T-shirt covering her body and turned off the lamp beside her bed. She tried to push Van Damme into a night closet for Abagail to torture until dawn. Since Mimi's purring and rubbing caused him discomfort, she'd throw in the cat for free. She'd release him in the morning, check his fingers for calculator burn and send him on his way.

Irish punched her violet-patterned pillowcase, then rolled over and jerked her sheets up to her chin. She scowled at the pine-bough shadows sweeping across the tiny rosebud design of her wallpaper.

Max had prowled through the house after their walk, then returned from the basement holding a dusty bottle like a prize. His strong hand had grasped the neck of the bottle as though once he had something or someone in his grasp, he'd never let go. Strolling up to her, he'd lifted the amber bottle and a singular mocking eyebrow. "My favorite. If you're not saving it, I'll add it to my bill at a good price."

She hadn't resisted throwing darts at him. "You see things you actually like?"

His smile hadn't been nice. More like showing teeth before he used them. "I enjoy the finer things of life, and this wine is one of them. I've promised myself a treat after examining your cookie jar and shoe box. By the way, some customer credit-card numbers were expired."

He'd settled into his room with the bottle of wine and her receipts to systemize Abagail's.

Irish kicked the bed in a series of fast one-two's. "Ohhh!" She twisted again, turning onto her stomach, and felt the elastic on her worn briefs tear. Squirming out of them, Irish looked at the Colorado moonlit night beyond the inn. She found herself thinking of the dark lights in Max's eyes as he'd sliced away at her ability to own and manage Abagail's.

When Max baited her, those dark eyes almost had a glint of humor.

"He's out to get me, "she whispered to the great horned owl soaring across the silvery moon. Inhaling the fresh air touched with scents of lavender, peonies and pine, Irish tried to pry Van Damme from her thoughts.

The roof outside her open window creaked. Then a man's shadowy body slid into her room. "Hello, little lady," Boonie rasped, the scent of whiskey clinging to him. "You waiting for me?"

"Boonie, you get out of here!" Irish tried to keep her voice low as Boonie sauntered to her bed. Though Irish knew she could manage him, she didn't want her guests disturbed.

"No city dude takes Boonie Riggs's woman away," he whispered drunkenly as he leaned over her head. "I saw the way he looked at you. I suppose that little walk to the barn had a real hot reason."

Irish took a deep steadying breath. Van Damme had looked at her as though she were unable to tie a bow, let alone run a health spa and inn. He'd drained a large amount of her patience. But her guests needed quiet, and Irish snagged the strength to deal with Boonie. She tried to remember that this neighboring rancher was a nice man, battling a series of bad financial and personal times.

She slid across the bed from him and stood. "Boonie, I've enjoyed our talks, and you've been welcome to come to the inn. But I'm not your woman."

Boonie lunged and sprawled across the bed. When he moved to come toward her, Irish backed toward the door. "Boonie Riggs, you get yourself under control," she managed shakily, spotting his drunken leer. "I'm just going to open this door, and you're going to walk out of the inn. You come back when you feel better. I'll bake your favorite gooey hot fudge cake—"

Boonie stepped toward her, leering full force. "I got better ideas for dessert, honey."

When he reached for her, Irish opened the door and stepped through it. Closing it, she gripped the crystal knob with both hands just as Boonie tried to pry it open. "Hush, Boonie. You'll wake up the guests."

Max frowned at his closed door; he wouldn't allow the hushed demanding noises beyond it to wrench him from

Rachmaninoff. He turned up the volume on his cassette player slightly. "Big mice," he stated tersely, wanting to ignore everything but the excellent bouquet of the fine wine and the wholesome scents of the Colorado night air. Rachmaninoff's movements wrapped around him soothingly, a Band-Aid on Irish's financial nightmares.

Not that Irish cared about profit statements.

Max scowled at the dark red wine, thinking about Irish. A rhapsody in smiles and sunlight, an upbeat personality who drew people to her without trying. J.D. had said that if Irish's TLC could be bottled, it would solve the world's problems.

Irish Dalton was an element Max did not want in his life. Maybe that was why he'd baited her earlier.

Lounging in his untied short satin robe, Max allowed the cool air to drift over his body. He swirled the wine thoughtfully, then rested the glass on his bare chest. He didn't like the sexual tension in his body, and he didn't like knowing that Irish had been the woman to fire it. He didn't like remembering how he had slashed at her about the conditions of the inn. And he didn't like remembering the vulnerable expression on her soft face when he'd mentioned animal cruelty. He'd felt as if he'd deliberately squashed a fluffy soufflé. Or a woman with a very tender heart.

Irish probably didn't have any idea about the animals' condition, though she obviously loved them.

Sipping the tart wine, Max rolled the taste on his tongue, savoring it. Glancing at his microcomputer on the antique cherrywood table serving as his desk, Max inhaled deeply. He'd filed Irish's bills and receipts away in a box beneath his large brass bed. With any luck, he wouldn't have to open that blitz of horrors again.

Another crash sounded in the hall, and Irish's muffled voice hissed, "Boonie, now I mean it! Be quiet! You'll wake up the guests. What about poor Mr. Essery who's recovering from a heart attack?"

Boonie returned something in outraged tones. Apparently his current problems overrode Mr. Essery's.

Max sighed and tried to place the feuding lovers at a distance while he enjoyed the sensuality of the cool air drifting over him.

Lovers? Max repeated mentally as the scuffle in the hall continued to grow louder. Max frowned, gulped down the wine he had been savoring and quickly tied his robe.

Startled to find himself jerking open his door, Max stepped into the hall to find the back of Irish's soft warm body thrust against his cool one.

With both hands grasping the knob to her bedroom door, Irish looked over her shoulder at him. Her eyes were wide and vulnerable, and Max reacted instantly. He took hold of the doorknob with one hand. To hold the knob and keep danger from Irish was instinctive. In that instant, she was his to protect. He circled Irish possessively with his free arm, drawing her into the protection of his body.

In the firm grasp of his hand, the doorknob rattled and shook while Boonie's muffled curses sounded on the opposite side. From Max's room, Rachmaninoff's romantic movements poured into the hallway. The ebb and tide of the emotional music wove around them, creating an intimacy Max hadn't experienced for years.

But Max couldn't move.

Max couldn't breathe.

Max couldn't think about anything but Irish looking up at him. A purple pansy nuance shaded her dark blue eyes, and a thick fringe of golden lashes framed the rounded shape. *An innocent,* Max thought absently, free-falling into a field of soft purple pansy petals. At odds with Irish's virginal expression, the sweet flow of her round body down the hardening warming length of his triggered an anticipation of melodious slow passion with incredible heights.

Her hands gently parted the gape of his robe and fluttered on his bare chest.

Violins quivered delicately in the Rachmaninoff strains, wrapping Max in Irish's magical soothing warmth.

Irish needed protection and care, gentleness and understanding. Yet at the same time, he could feel a passion within her that could melt away his emptiness.

Max instinctively drew her tighter against him. Opening his free hand to fit into the neat curve of her waist and hip, Max savored the rounded feminine line with a slow caress. His fingers smoothed a bare soft hip, splaying gently across the satiny skin.

"Oh," she whispered, her fingers widening on his chest.

Locked together, Max felt her every breath. Felt the rise and fall of her breasts against his stomach, felt himself being absorbed by her scents of lavender and mountain meadow flowers. Of sunshine and warmth.

Pressed intimately against her thighs, Max forgot about the rattling noise. He lowered his lips to fit slowly, carefully over her parted soft ones and felt himself slide into a lush field of clover and daisies and Irish.

As if testing his favorite wine, Max nibbled slowly at the delicate curve of her mouth, savoring the fresh sweet taste. Like buttery croissants with strawberry preserves....

She moved against him slightly, lifting and parting her lips, and Max widened his stance to support her weight, drowning in the sensations her response aroused. Gathering her closer, Max slid his hand higher under her T-shirt until he found her breast.

The delightful nub responded to his circling fingertip. So soft, he decided distantly, smoothing the satiny skin. Soft and warm. She'd give him everything. He'd give her more.

Aligned with her body, Max deepened the kiss, lowering his hand to press her hips nearer. He absently let go of the doorknob and wrapped his free hand around the back of her neck.

Then Boonie jerked open the door.

"Now ain't this nice?" Boonie asked, leering at Irish's flushed and confused face. "Hey! What's that funny music?"

Gripping her possessively closer, Max was stunned by the hunger and anger washing over him. Boonie's leer needed to be shoved...

Max hesitated for a fraction of a second, torn between cramming the leer down Boonie's throat and lingering in Irish's warmth and softness.

Then he moved quickly, thrusting Irish behind him as he grasped Boonie's wrist, levering it behind him. "Come along," he gritted between his teeth. "Anyone who doesn't recognize Rachmaninoff needs to say good-night."

Boonie managed a "Hey!" before Max clamped his hand over the cowboy's mouth. He moved Boonie through the hallway, down the stairs and out the front door without a sound.

"Oh, my," Irish said softly, placing her fingers over her well-kissed lips as she watched Max move Boonie quietly down the hall. Max's mouth had tasted of pungent sweet wine. He'd kissed her with tender hunger, exploring and examining every texture and flavor as though her mouth was a delicate aperitif.

Irish swallowed, remembering how his body had fitted intimately to hers. Wrapped in his arms and the beautiful music, Irish had felt as though she were in the arms of her beloved....

"Oh, my," she repeated as her other hand flattened low on her stomach to control the warmth surging there. She closed her eyes, trying to dislodge the memory.

Boonie's truck sputtered and lunged out into the quiet night as Irish moved into her room and closed the door. She crawled into her bed, arranged the sun-scented sheet safely over her and crossed her folded hands upon her chest. Her heartbeat would eventually return to normal. Maybe.

She turned to stare at the moonbeams slipping through the pine boughs outside her window.

Max had wanted her desperately. With tenderness. With consuming passion. As if she had been made for him alone. As if she was uniquely his to care for.

Breathing quietly, she relived Max's every touch. The slow warmth of his safe hands exploring her curves as if he found her exciting. She touched her breasts with her fingertips, remembering how he had gently caressed and supported their weight. She found tears creeping down her cheeks and she sniffed, wiping her eyes with a corner of the sheet.

A hallway board creaked, and her door swung open. From the hall, Max asked huskily, "Are you all right, Irish?"

"Fine," she managed, wishing her voice was more steady.

"Fine," he repeated grimly, closing the door and walking toward the bed. "Boonie is gone. Did he hurt you?"

The edge to his low voice reminded Irish of Max's savage expression as he'd leveled his attention on Boonie. "Did you hurt him?" she asked, drying her cheek on the pillowcase.

"Let's say I gave him something to think about." Behind her the mattress gave way to Max's weight. His hand found her shoulder in the darkness. "He won't be back. Did he hurt you?" he asked again, more urgently this time, his voice slightly rough.

"No." She was suddenly cold, and startled to find herself longing for the warmth of Max's arms.

Max rubbed her shoulder awkwardly as though he wasn't used to giving comfort. When she turned to him, the moonlight slipping through the window outlined his harsh expression.

He looked so worried, so alone in the silvery light. So angry and primitive. "I'm fine," she murmured again, after a tense moment when Max's fingers strayed to her collarbone, tracing the smooth skin.

He inhaled, his fingertips trembling as they passed over her arm. "Should I call Granny or Nadia for you?"

"I'm really okay, Max. You can go now." She didn't want him to see her cry, and his uncertainty had brought her to the brink.

"I suppose we'll have to deal with what happened earlier," he began roughly, searching her face in the square of moonlight lying across her pillow. "Look, Irish, I don't grab women in the middle of the night...."

Irish found herself placing her hand behind his neck. For a moment he resisted the gentle tug, then allowed himself to be brought gently down to her. Irish smiled softly. Against his cheek, rough with evening stubble, she whispered, "Don't worry so, Max. I wasn't hurt. Thank you...."

Max's head turned slightly until their lips barely touched and neither could move. "Look, Irish...I was out of bounds," he said huskily after a long moment.

"Stop apologizing, Max," she returned softly, stroking the taut back of his neck. He wasn't as cool as he appeared. A thrill soared through Irish. Max, it seemed, was not exactly in control of himself.

Rattling Max's perfect image and discovering his wonderful kisses had inflated her ego. Irish hadn't seen herself as a desirable woman. She smiled against his mouth, kissing him delicately. "Are you going to kiss me back?" she teased after a moment.

Max shivered. His breath was ragged, his skin heating to her touch. "Poor Max," she soothed, meaning it as she rubbed her cheek against his. "You've had a bad day, haven't you?"

He swallowed at that, muttering darkly, "I should be getting the hell out of here before it's too late...."

Because he needed her touch, Irish locked both her arms around him and drew him down against her. She loved the hard steely feel of his bare chest. She loved the rapid thumping of his heart and the way his mouth moved cautiously against her temple.

She rubbed the ridges of his back muscles, kneading the tense line of his shoulders.

Then Max kissed her fully. When the steamy sensuous kiss ended, he braced his hands on either side of her pillow and whispered roughly, "We should..."

In the shadows above her, Max looked distracted, hot and rumpled. And very much in need of her. Irish felt the answering heat race through her and she reached for him.

For an instant he rested against her, tense and trembling. "You're so soft, Irish," he said unevenly, levering himself onto the bed slowly. He lay full length against her, his hand running lightly over her body covered by the sheet. His touch trembled and sought, leaving her wondering....

"Come here," she whispered back, knowing he would.

"Irish," he protested in a low rough tone, just before settling his mouth over hers.

When Max lifted the sheet aside, and his trembling hands drew her against him, she could stop him with a touch, with a murmur.

When his robe followed Irish's shirt to the floor, Max knew he should stop. There was danger in relationships, pain in wanting to be needed and healed and caressed. But her warmth tangled like sunlight in the shadowy ache he'd carried for years, and he found himself seeking more.

Sliding into her heat, Max found what he had wanted, what he'd needed for a lifetime. She took him deeper, settling him into a soft tangle of arms and legs.

Max gave himself to her keeping, swept by the need to cherish and bind her to him, to care.

When their passion deepened, Max found her soft cries snaring him deeper, melting something long ago buried. Trapped on a heated pinnacle, Max gave himself to her.

An instant later, with Irish's body trembling beneath his, he realized she'd found that same desperate pleasure.

The second wave of passion caught him unprepared, washing over him before the first had allowed him to settle. He caught Irish to him, knowing that nothing else mattered but this moment of heat and softness.

Max's last thought before he drifted off to sleep, tangled in the warmth of Irish's scent and softness, was that he'd entered a magical kingdom of whimsy, tenderness and fire.

In her arms, he'd experienced a moment in time so fragile and wonderful that he didn't want to dissect it.

Three

Just before dawn, the soft coo of a dove drifted through the open window of Irish's bedroom.

Morning floated around Max like a silken feather, dusting, brushing, tantalizing. The cool air toyed in the folds of the lacy sheer curtain and slid through the hair covering his chest like a lover's seeking fingers. Keeping his eyes closed, Max allowed himself to drift in the moment and in the scents of mountain pine and lavender. Upon waking, his body was usually tense, ready to spring into the day; but this special morning, a lazy contentment spread throughout his muscles like a warmed berry syrup over fresh crepes.

Max slid his hand to caress the long smooth warmth curled next to him beneath the sheet. The night and the woman had become one—soft and powerful, magical and passionate—wrapping him in an ecstasy he'd never experienced before. He'd found the softness as powerfully exciting as the driving hot need she'd answered. The night had been a Tchaikovsky overture, pacing slow sweet desire into a rising demanding passion filled with husky whispers and sighs.

Max stretched, smiling as his palm found the smoothly rounded feminine thigh and slowly, luxuriously, traced the contours.

He wanted to loll on the sheets, to wallow in the lingering sweet taste of the night—now that he had found what he wanted.

Feeling pleased with himself, Max turned his head on the pillow. He nuzzled the silky strands clinging to his morning beard, inhaling the tantalizing scents as his hand leisurely explored the smooth curves shifting comfortably against his side.

Max turned slightly, adjusting more fully to the breasts settling softly against his chest. Their bodies folded together naturally, fitting perfectly.

He drifted along drowsily, clinging to the enchantment and knowing that he had never been more satisfied than at this moment. Smiling lazily, Max caressed the gentle indentation of a woman's waist. The soft thigh draped across his moved, sliding experimentally as her insole caressed his calf.

Max sighed, grinning slightly while he lingered in the elusive fragrance of the night's lovemaking. As he lingered in his pleasure, his grin widened. It would happen again. He knew in another moment they would be exploring each other tenderly; her sweet kisses would cause the fiery hunger, and the muffled startled sounds she'd make would storm his senses.

Exploring fingers toyed with the hair on his chest, smoothed it as though she were stroking a kitten. And Max thought of his youthful dream to spend a week in bed with a woman. Somehow he never had. Now the possibility seemed likely—

Max inhaled sharply, his heart beating more quickly. Her fingers skimmed his shoulders, and her breath swept across his nipple, sensitizing it and stirring other sensuous realms as she sighed in her sleep.

He shivered slightly, wrapped in the knowledge that Irish was the most responsive passionate woman he'd ever known. She'd given him honesty, a seductress who snared him with her magic and held him in her power.

Irish?

Max's lids opened, the sunlight blinding him just as a rooster crowed in all his male glory.

Who the hell was Irish? He'd only met her yesterday.

Fully awake now, Max forced his fingers to still just before closing possessively over her breast. He frowned and lifted his hand away as an enticing hardening nub brushed his palm. Trying to calm himself while her fingers were skimming the hair on his chest, Max replaced his hand carefully on the sheets and gripped them for an anchor. He tried to place himself into the *now* time zone.

He forced a hard swallow as the rooster crowed again, boasting his male powers. Max inhaled sharply, catching Irish's scents. They'd made love three times, *and he hadn't used protection*. He'd acted like a hot-blooded boy, hungry and careless of the results.

Max shut his eyes against the sight of the morning sun tripping across the tiny roses on the wallpaper. Last night, Irish had taken him into a tenderness he'd never experienced and into equatorial passions he'd never had stirred.

Max scowled at the gay rosebuds. He didn't want his passions stirred. A woman like Irish was trouble.

Chancing a glance at her, Max winced slightly at the sight of her well-kissed mouth. On her throat were tiny marks caused by his beard. She looked soft and loved—and inviting. The need to wake her with a kiss rose wildly in him, almost frightening in its power.

The morning breeze swept across his sweaty forehead, cooling it. He closed his eyes, fighting off a whimsical plan for the next time they made love; it had everything to do with changing positions on the sheets scented of the Colorado sun. Of fitting silky skin and freckles over his body in lieu of a sheet.

Of finding that sensitive spot just behind her ear and waiting for the delightful silken quivers....

A dull headache began to throb at the back of his head when he remembered Irish's breathless startled cries blending with the soft sound of his laughter.

The vein along Max's right temple pounded. *He'd never chuckled in his life.*

Max's fingers curled into fists. Irish wasn't a well-integrated business system; she was magic and softness, like an iridescent soap bubble flying high on the mountain winds and catching the sun.

A relationship would be disaster for them.

Slowly, carefully, Max eased his body away from her care. Then he stood alone in the cold morning air and shivered.

Placing the unbaked cinnamon rolls on the cookie sheet, Irish avoided Nadia's curious glances. Irish flushed each time the fortune-teller looked her way.

This morning wasn't filled with loving promises and sweet nibbling kisses. Things just weren't perking along like they should be after a wonderful night, and Irish resented the emptiness she'd carried since Max had uncoiled himself from her side. She ached in unfamiliar muscles, and her heart felt as though it had been sliced.

Boonie had called earlier, apologizing in muffled tones. With one blow, Max had given the rancher black eyes, a swollen nose and a split lip. According to Boonie, Max lacked "good-old-boy class" and was a "city animal from hell." In lieu of a legal suit, Boonie had settled for his favorite hot fudge cake, delivered to his doorstep safely away from Max.

Max.

She nibbled at her lip, wincing at the tenderness. Max had stood over her in the dawn, watching her for an eternity as she'd feigned sleep. His hand had trembled when he'd stroked a tendril away from her cheek, and she'd wanted to open her arms to him again.

She'd wanted to feel the safety of his strong arms wrapped around her, the husky low intimate sound of his voice soothing her again. Shy of him in the cool morning, Irish had waited for the moment when he'd kiss her. Max's kisses were startling—reverent, magical, lazy, hot and hungry.

Instead he had covered her bare shoulder with the sheet, smoothed back a curl from her cheek and had slipped from her room. Like a night shadow sliding from the reality of dawn.

Clinging to his scent, she had moved into the warm space he had vacated. *Max.*

In the kitchen, Irish opened the oven door to check the temperature. Satisfied by the heat swirling around her, she closed the door and thought of Max's cold scowl.

How could Max love her so tenderly in the magical night, then scowl at her over the rim of his morning coffee cup? His dark glance had not missed her flushed face as she'd passed him with a tray of blueberry muffins. He'd been lounging against the kitchen door, dressed in Armani slacks and a matching shirt. He'd slipped back into his calculator-for-a-heart image, and his hard expression had made her ache. "I'll need to wash my car. But then you probably know that," he had said ominously.

Remembering the tender night heat, she'd wanted to fold herself to him, kiss the tiny razor cut and offer to help wash the bird droppings from his car. But Max had looked as thunderous as a high mountain storm, his mouth grim. "Can you fit me into your schedule? We need to talk."

His impersonal tone had scraped on her uncertain nerves like a nail drawn down a blackboard, and she'd found an excuse to move away from him.

In her usual morning scramble to prepare breakfast, Irish resented the happy chatter around her. Granny and the guests moved comfortably between the kitchen and the dining room, serving themselves blueberry pancakes, fruit and bran.

Irish experimentally probed her sensitive lips with the tip of her tongue. She felt coiled like the cinnamon rolls she'd just thrust into the oven. She wanted to pommel Max with blueberry muffins at five paces.

A musical jingle of bangle bracelets signaled Nadia's arrival at her side. The fortune-teller nudged Irish. "Ah, the black knight who protected your honor arrives with his notebook. His face looks like cold steel."

"I didn't need protection from Boonie," Irish muttered, ignoring the amused slide of Nadia's eyes down to the whisker burns on her neck.

Max walked into the kitchen as Irish was scooping brown sugar into a bowl, and she steeled herself to look up at him. She shivered, reminded of the way the hair on his chest had tickled her bare back as he'd drawn her tightly against him.

She shivered again as she remembered Max's tongue tracking a spot he'd discovered just behind her ear.

"Interesting," Nadia murmured lightly before drifting away in a tinkle of bracelets and charms. "I shall ask Madame Abagail's opinion of the event...."

Nadia's voice was overlaid by Max's impatient growl. "Well?" Max demanded coolly. "When can we schedule a conference? Nine o'clock?"

Irish plopped the lid on the sugar bowl. Max's business-like tone had ignited shimmering little sparks of anger. Maybe he could stuff the magical night into a briefcase, but she couldn't.

Irish didn't like feeling angry. And she didn't like the quick efficient way Max checked her name on his notebook's list. *Why wasn't he holding her and kissing her with those tender rough hungry kisses and touching her with trembling hands and growling contentedly in her ear, and—*

A new wave of anger crashed over her. The night-after equation called for Max's tongue seeking that excitable spot behind her ear.

Her ex-fiancé hadn't discovered that spot. She hadn't known it existed. If Max was going to discover her sensitive responsive areas, the least he could do was to use them....

"I have enough notes to lay out a sensible system," Max stated. "If you can schedule—" he glanced at his wristwatch "—twenty-five minutes, we can discuss an efficiency system. You need an alarm unit. I'll contract people to instruct you on the fine points. I can point out a few discrepancies in Jeff's receipts, then you can find the rest of the errors yourself." Max's firm lips pressed together for an instant before he continued grimly, "And the other *matter* needs to be clarified, too."

His eyes drifted over her flour-dusted T-shirt, and Irish returned the cool look, crossing her arms protectively over her chest. Tuned to Max's hard length, her body ached to throw itself into his arms. But Max's scowl wasn't welcoming; Max-in-the-morning—the morning *after*—wasn't exactly a sweetheart.

Something dark and nasty roamed in the depths of his eyes, accusing her of seduction. Irish wanted to sling the accusation back at him. How did he explain the husky encouragements he'd murmured against her skin? Feeling betrayed, Irish acknowledged the basis of her newly discovered temper. Max had no business ruining something so beautiful.

Looking at the open collar of his shirt and allowing her gaze to stroll down, then back up the neat crease in his slacks, she said, "You're referring to last night as the 'matter,' I suppose? Is last night on your checklist, too?"

Max seemed to grind his teeth momentarily before he said tightly, "You're going to be difficult, aren't you?"

Irish's eyebrows lifted, her cold smile concealing the emotions racing through her. Max might slip from night lover to morning beast easily, but not without a tap on his arrogant nose. "You want to tear my business apart and suck the juice out, Max. What do you expect?"

"Be reasonable, Irish," he snapped after inhaling sharply. He glanced at Nadia, who was nibbling on an orange slice. When the fortune-teller smiled benignly back at him, Max lowered his voice. "You're emotional, and that's not good business—"

"Outside," she ordered, wondering how Max would look floundering fully dressed in the cold green clay of the beauty bog. "You have until the cinnamon rolls are done."

Irish wiped her hands on a dish towel and tossed it onto the counter. Max glanced at his watch. "Twenty minutes?"

"Does your heart run on a clock, too, Max? When the rolls are done, I'll take them out," she snapped, startling herself.

Stepping into the morning sun, Irish realized she had never been so angry. For once she ignored the scented herbs along the bricked pathway. She shook off Max's hand as it cupped her elbow, only to find her wrist encircled by his unrelenting fingers. "Irish," Max said under his breath, "emotion does not help the situation."

At the beauty bog, Irish jerked her wrist free and glared up at him. "Emotion? Now why would I be emotional? Because I find myself in bed with every man who stays here? Do you think I'm under Abagail's lovemaking-versus-stress influence?"

A tinge of red moved upward from Max's throat, staining his dark cheeks. "Don't. Just don't," he ordered tightly.

He shifted uncomfortably as Irish tried to continue glaring up at him. It was difficult to do with tears burning her eyes and a sob clogging her tight throat. Cupid's arrow did hurt, she thought wildly, bracing herself as the chubby little winged monster started a flurry of painful little pings into her heart.

Max glanced at her face just as a tear oozed from the corner of her eye. He swallowed, then looked away, scanning the grassy foothills of the mountains. He shifted restlessly, locking his legs in an uncompromising stance, then pinned her with his stare. "If it's any comfort, I didn't expect last night, either. Sex isn't something I jump into lightly. But it's been a long time—that and the wine—and because you'd just had a frightening experience... Maybe it was a reaction on both our parts."

"Sex?" Irish repeated blankly and wondered how something so beautiful could be jammed into three letters. She swallowed, mentally tossing the poetry she had expected into the trash basket.

So he wanted to rationalize and dissect every beautiful moment they'd spent in the night, did he? She'd known exactly what she was doing—caring for him. And he'd merely needed someone for a midnight aperitif? What was she, the maraschino cherry on top of a sundae? A shell plucked from a sandy beach? A... Irish blinked against the tears misting her eyes. "So I had a reaction from a frightening experience," she repeated carefully through her teeth. "Or overdosed on that classical stuff coming from your room. Whatever happened to old-fashioned rock and roll? And of course I jump into bed with every Tom, Dick—"

She wasn't prepared for the savagery in his expression, nor the quick way he moved to draw her into the shadows of the weeping willow and away from curious eyes. "You're not making this easy for either one of us," Max said roughly, scanning her swollen lips. "It happened and that's it."

"You practically broke poor Boonie's nose," she accused, struggling against him.

"That idiot," Max snapped. "He's damned lucky I didn't break his legs."

"Boonie is a friend!" Irish began hotly, ignoring the way Max tenderly brushed her hair away from her cheek. His eyes narrowed, tracking the whisker burns on her pale throat. She swatted at his hand as it lingered over her hot skin, testing the tiny evidence of the long sweet night. "You're not going to interfere by setting up computers beeping and blinking all over the place. And I won't have people run down for unpaid bills when they're dealing with enough stress. You're not dragging in gizmos and systems and trained staff to strip everything away... So you hadn't had sex for a time and you decided—"

"Irish, if you want to argue, do it logically. Stop skipping all over the main points and stay on track. You've got a houseful of people who don't pay their way. Jeff is playing you for a fool, and Jonathan needs to be thrown out on his ear. Nadia could use her spare time doing maid work. You need a computer system for record-keeping and credit references. You need an office with a resident bookkeeper to handle invoices, and a telephone linkup with credit-card companies to check your guests' credit."

"And you need a heart in there," Irish interrupted hotly, jabbing him in the chest.

"I have a heart," Max said carefully, looming over her. "You're too emotional."

"You don't scare me, Mr. Whizmo-Gizmo," Irish said just before she thrust her open hands into his flat midsection. Max's eyes widened in surprise; his Italian loafers struggled for a firm spot on the cusp of the bog just before he sprawled backward into the green clay.

Irish dusted her hands together and smiled down at him. "You're fired, Max. You can wash your car elsewhere," she said cheerfully and, in her opinion, quite elegantly. Then another tear slid down her cheek and she sniffed.

Walking back to the inn, Irish slashed the back of her hand across her damp cheeks and muttered darkly, "I don't know, Abagail. Men just aren't what they used to be. What happened to poetry and violet nosegays and compliments and morning-after hugs?"

She hadn't sensed him near her, but suddenly, Max's goo-covered hands were gripping her upper arms, holding her still.

His lips drew back from his teeth in a smile that did not suit the fiery anger in his eyes. A drop of goo clung to his cheek. "If landing me in that mess made you feel better, I'm glad. It was childish, but knowing your logic, it's understandable," he stated tightly. "I'll clean up and have a summary file prepared for you within one hour and fifteen minutes. Try to concentrate on the differences in the bills Jeff has signed—he's skimming a neat margin from you. I'll send a copy to J.D., and he can reach me in Tahoe if he has questions."

He paused, deepened his scowl and added quietly, "If you have any problems because of last night—"

Fighting for her pride, Irish lashed out shakily, "I won't have problems from last night—I'm an adult. I can deal with a one-night stand just the same as you."

"I said it was a moment in time, caused by special circumstances—not a one-night stand," he stated darkly, anger flaring in his dark eyes. "I didn't use protection, Irish," Max reminded her quietly, watching the red heat crawl up her face. A muscle worked in his jaw as he continued, "At forty-two, I've never experienced a ticking biological clock, Irish. I'm usually very careful, but the circumstances—"

"Usually?" she repeated blankly. "So you aren't in practice and you goofed?"

The harsh lines bordering Max's mouth deepened, and his lips pressed together. "Don't worry, Irish. Chances are you aren't pregnant. According to my parents who are genetic experts, the likelihood of pregnancy the first time are fifty to one."

Releasing her carefully, Max reached to remove a clinging leaf from her hair. He slipped off his muddy Italian loafers, and a moment later, the Armani slacks clung to his backside as he walked stiffly into the inn carrying his shoes.

When Irish finally recovered from Max's quiet implication that she could be carrying his baby, she shivered. "Not a chance," she whispered unevenly to the light breeze. "This isn't Las Vegas and I don't have to beat fifty-to-one odds."

Irish eased out of bed. She hadn't slept well since last week's enlightening experience with Max and his morning revelation that she could be pregnant. Her breasts were tender, and unable to sleep on her stomach, she'd tossed about restlessly during the night. Forcing herself to her feet, Irish heard the rooster crow. "Oh, shut up," she muttered, padding to the bathroom.

On her way back to bed, she glanced at Max's summary file lying unopened on the cherrywood dresser.

Max hadn't called, she realized wearily, as she put on her jeans. So much for the second romantic interlude in her life. Maxwell Van Damme was probably in Tahoe, puttering with gizmos.

She closed her eyes, shutting out the image in the bureau mirror. She looked just like she felt, aching and tired, her soul bruised. She'd reacted shrewishly to Max, and that knowledge hadn't helped her temperament.

After her affair with Mark, she'd managed to salvage her pride and dignity. Max had stirred her temper, and she didn't appreciate it.

Drawing on her bra, Irish loosened the clasp from its usual setting to ease the tightness. She frowned, studying her mirrored image. She'd lost weight in the past couple of months; the waistband of her jeans had been steadily loosening. Yet her bustline— "It's not possible," she said firmly, shaking her head and returning to the bathroom.

Later, Irish stood at the kitchen window and studied the dew clinging to a spider web. She held a bowl of pancake batter against her, whipping the mixture with a wooden spoon and staring intently at the tiny watery jewels.

She missed Max.

Irish absently traced the spider's path, bypassing the droplets on her way to the center of the web. Without a backward glance, Max had swooped out of Kodiac in his gleaming bird-spotted car. In his wake, clouds of dust had billowed, then settled slowly.

She gripped the big mixing bowl tighter, thinking of the possibility of a baby—a tiny reminder of Max, tucked safely away....

"Not a chance," she whispered uneasily as she set the bowl on the counter.

But then she remembered that night and the way Max had loved her—repeatedly. As though he needed her to live. Counting carefully until the next month, Irish marked a big red X on the kitchen calendar.

In the safety of her room three weeks later, Irish stared at the positive results of her home pregnancy test. She tilted the tube and blinked. "Well, maybe," she whispered. "Just maybe."

The next week, Irish marked a steady line through the second week on the June calendar. The inn was filled, and while she dealt with the needs of her customers, she thought about the reality of having a baby. She wanted one desperately, and now the idea had been presented to her à la Van Damme. All the forgotten dreams of children came dancing back on the wisp of a fifty-to-one chance. "Mommy? Mama?" she tested while grinning happily at the children racing through the meadow.

The baby was hers alone, she decided firmly. Max, who'd zoomed out of the Rockies in full regal male potency, had gifted her with the possibility of a child. In the privacy of the morning, she lingered in bed and dreamed about the tiny life within her. Max had a unique part in the conception, but he didn't need to know or feel obligated. Since she'd gotten him out of the dugouts and back into the game, he was probably practicing his batting average *with protection.*

She deeply wanted the baby. Wanted to love him and watch him grow. She grinned, running her hand over her abdomen for the hundredth time.

Then Irish's first wave of nausea swept over her.

Max parked his Porsche a safe distance away from the birds' roosting tree. At seven in the morning, the July air was cool and filled with enticing scents of freshly baked bread and coffee. He ran his hand through his hair and muttered, "What the hell am I doing back here?"

Irish had been dancing through his mind for two months; he didn't like the coldness shrouding him since meeting her. Pushed to the edge, Max had had enough. He'd driven all night to the passionate strains of Tchaikovsky's *Romeo and Juliet* overture.

Max ran his hand along his unshaven jaw. He wasn't used to sleepless nights and dreams of sweet loving impish blondes. During the days, Irish in the sun, Irish in the sensuous night skipped happily through his thoughts. She'd destroyed his concentration, entering his systems layouts for the Tahoe resort project. His assignment was a success, but Max wouldn't be able to work on another high-tech project until he put Irish in her proper place—well away from his emotions.

If only he could stop seeing her pansy-blue eyes filled with tears...

Mimi came running out, purring and nuzzling his legs until he stopped to rub the spot behind her ears.

When Max entered the foyer, Nadia smiled widely, as though she knew something he didn't, and pointed a ruby-encrusted finger toward the dining room. Max nodded grimly at Granny and Link, who looked at him as though he were a suspect returning to the scene of the crime. Then he spotted Boonie, seated at the breakfast table and buttering a fluffy biscuit just past a bouquet of daisies and delicate bleeding hearts.

Max stopped in midstride, fighting his rising anger as the rooster crowed outside in the July sun. The tiny red bleeding hearts shimmered quietly in a patch of sunlight as Max thought about the satisfaction he'd gotten from dealing with Boonie. "Hello," he said quietly, pleased that Boonie paled and touched his healed nose.

The new guests smiled, welcoming him as Irish entered carrying a platter of sourdough biscuits. "Max!"

Max glanced at Boonie who was excusing himself, then he smiled at Irish. Dressed in jeans and a tight Mickey Mouse T-shirt, she looked as inviting as the freshly baked biscuits. Max forced down the whimsical thought of how he'd like to honey and butter her. "Irish. I came back to check on your progress with my recommendations. How are you?"

She'd changed, he decided as she stared back at him. Those wide blue eyes had darkened, their depths mysterious. Her mouth, caught in a wide smile, needed to be kissed. Max's gaze slid unerringly down her body, lingering on her breasts. Fuller now, they thrust against Mickey's ears.

"I thought I fired you," she began hotly, just before the biscuits slid to the floor and she fainted into Max's arms.

Granny plucked the platter from Irish's limp grasp, muttering, "Happens like that sometimes, I guess. First time for her... Don't just stand there—carry her on upstairs, Max. I reckon you two need to be alone."

"Get a doctor—" he ordered.

"Huh! *You* may need one. Irish will be fine."

Nadia winked as Max carried Irish's limp body past her. "Ah, love," she sighed in his wake.

Running up the stairs, Max took care not to jostle Irish. Lowering her to her bed, he placed a cold wet cloth on her forehead just as she began stirring. "Irish?" he heard himself say just as her eyes opened and she stared blankly up at him.

"Max, what are you doing here?" she asked huskily.

He brushed a curl away from her cheek, noting her pale color and the damp sheen of sweat on her forehead. "You're not well, Irish. Have you seen a doctor?"

She stared blankly at him for a moment, groaned, then turned on her side away from him. The cloth on her forehead slipped, and Max sat on the bed, holding it in place. "Irish?"

"Go away," she said unevenly. "Go back to your gizmo kingdom. Get lost...the birds are circling your car... Morticia's teeth have been cleaned...'Bye."

"Try that rubbish on Boonie. He's dense enough to buy it," Max said just as unevenly and wondered when his heart had started beating again. He rubbed her back and found the muscles tense beneath his hand. "Irish, have you seen a doctor?" he repeated.

He couldn't remember terror and now it had found him, impaling him on the point of a giant cold knife.

"I'm not up to a Maxwell Van Damme moment just now," she whispered brokenly, and Max's stomach lurched. "Go bother a computer or something."

After a brief knock on the door, Granny entered the room carrying a glass of milk and a plate of crackers. She placed them on the bedside table, then scowled at Max as though he'd axed her favorite rooster. "Men. They get off easy. It's us womenfolk that bear the burdens. Have her eat the crackers and lie still for a minute. Morning sickness usually passes fast enough."

"Morning sickness?" Max rapped out sharply, his eyes slashing down at Irish. "Morning sickness as in *you're pregnant?*"

Irish groaned, pulled a pillow over her head and groaned again. "You should know, young man." Granny sniffed airily, then glared at Max and marched stiffly from the room.

Max stared at the crackers, then back at Irish. "Granny wants you to eat the crackers," he said, feeling a little woozy. Max chalked his unsettled nausea up to the long drive and the passionate strains of *Romeo and Juliet*.

He found Irish's limp hand. Fitted within his, her hand seemed small and fragile. "Morning sickness?" he repeated shakily as a cold damp sweat broke out on his forehead.

Max calculated quickly backward while his stomach threatened to lurch again. "Irish, you're pregnant...."

"Isn't anything private? Suppose I'm high on cinnamon fumes or catnip?" Irish returned shakily, turning her head toward him. Her eyes widened, searching his face. "Max? Are you sick?" she asked as he stretched out beside her, his free hand resting on his forehead.

"Just a little upset stomach...no, I'm hot...no, I'm cold," he said raggedly, turning his head to her.

Irish was beautiful, he thought hazily as she patted the cold damp cloth around his face. And worried about him. Her blue eyes were filled with concern, her fingers cool on his sweaty brow. If only the mushroom-and-bacon omelet he'd eaten earlier this morning wasn't rolling around in his stomach, he'd... Absently Max wondered what he would do. Somehow he seemed adrift in a soothing warm joyous pansy-petaled lake.

No one had ever really worried about him. "You're pregnant," he said quietly, letting the cool shadows of the room absorb the wonder he had begun to experience.

"Max, *I'm* going to have *my* baby," Irish said softly, reaching for a cracker.

He shivered, trying to dislodge the woozy clammy feeling. "Stop rocking the bed," he ordered, then attempted a smile as he explained, "I've been driving all night and I'm a little bit off balance.... You'll be a perfect mother, by the way."

Irish didn't return the grin. She glared at him warily while she nibbled her cracker. "Don't get any big ideas, Max."

He blinked, noting with satisfaction that his weak moment had passed. He wanted to nibble that tiny cracker crumb from her lips. "As the father, I have a certain interest in the matter. Have you seen a doctor? I'll have him checked out."

"Max," she warned, rubbing her hand across her flat stomach. "When I choose a doctor, you are not included in the decision. No one is asking anything of you. You have no obligations. I can manage."

Max replaced her hand with his, easing up under her T-shirt and beneath her jeans. Between them and the magical night, they had created a tiny life. It lay vulnerable and sleeping within Irish's soft body. She'd kiss every bruise and play games on rainy days. She'd be perfect while he... Max frowned, thinking of his childhood. *Would he be able to give a child the love it needed?*

Max grinned sheepishly, feeling as though he could leap over the Rockies like Superman. "I'll work up a Mendelian—a genetic chart. I'll need facts about your family. I'll set up charts and do probability sheets on the new computer—"

"I haven't ordered a new gizmo, Max. Back off," Irish ordered fiercely, easing herself from the bed to stand looking down at him.

Max wanted to tug her back, to hold her against him and kiss the strawberry taste from her soft bottom lip. He wanted to say just the right things to soothe her, to tell her of his fears and the wonder bubbling inside him, but right now he couldn't find the strength. He placed the cold cloth back over his forehead. "We'll talk later, Irish."

"Maybe we will, and maybe we won't. You can stay until you feel better, Max, but then it's checkout time for you. Do you understand?"

Max took her tightly closed hand and brought it to his lips. He had other plans, but just now Irish wasn't feeling well. He turned the cold cloth over and wondered why the bed was swaying like a hammock. He blew a bothersome lavender pillow ruffle from his cheek. "Maybe I do, and maybe I don't."

"Ohhh!"

"The one thing that I do know, Irish," Max said solemnly, closing his eyes and holding her hand like a lifeline as the hammock swayed and the ruffle bothered, "is that I have no intentions of checking out of the scene. I'm responsible for the baby and you now. And I intend to be right here through everything."

"Max..." Irish had paled during his declaration, and she'd sat down on the violet-patterned coverlet. "You're not invited to the party. There is no need..."

But her fingers tightened within his, and Max took that as a small comfort. "Are you sick every morning? When did it start?" he asked, remembering that human pregnancy was divided into three parts called trimesters. "You'll need to write the sexes of the children in your family as far back as you can remember. I'll call Katherine to confirm.... Aren't you feeling well again?" Max asked, just as Irish lay down carefully beside him.

She took the cloth, placing it back on her own forehead. "Shut up, Max."

Max drew her limp hand to his chest and smiled serenely. "Daddy," he whispered aloud.

Irish groaned quietly beside him and Max grinned. "Daddy," he said again.

"Max..." Irish protested weakly.

He patted her hand as tiny happy pongs shot off in the region of his heart. Suddenly Max wanted to boast to someone, anyone. He wanted... he felt... Unable to dissect his emotions, Max settled for a big grin and gave Irish his first spontaneous hug. "I'm very happy," he whispered humbly against the softness of her hair.

She stiffened instantly, and Max fought the panic clawing at him. The words tore at his throat, tasted bitter on his lips, as he asked, "Do you want the baby, Irish?"

She ran her hand lovingly across her stomach. "More than I've ever wanted anything. Thank you, Max."

* * *

When Irish had thanked Max for blessing her with a baby, his smile had reminded her of a wolf coming to dinner. She'd thought of how he'd looked at Abagail's that fateful day—as if he'd lay out systems and lives to suit him. "You're welcome, Irish," he'd said. "But you're not thanking me politely, then shutting the door on me."

He'd eased from the bed to stand over her, and she'd had the fierce premonition that Max wasn't going anywhere.

For the rest of the day, she waited for Max to return from his appointment in Denver and in the late evening, the black Porsche soared out of the dusk and slid into an empty cattle-loafing shed.

Mimi came running around the corner of the house, racing toward the shed.

Irish stopped watering the hanging parsley baskets on the back porch when Max emerged from the shadows of the building. Dressed in a cream-colored cotton sweater and tight worn jeans, Max glanced at her, then began emptying the car. Mimi trotted along beside him, and at each pause she rubbed sensuously against his leg, then flopped on her back exposing her stomach to be scratched. Max stopped and obliged. Carrying bags and boxes to the small cottage behind the inn, Max ignored Irish's "Hey! What do you think you're doing?"

The cottage had served as Abagail's private love nest, and J.D. had used it while pursuing Katherine. The intimate mirror-lined house had occasionally been used by honeymooners, but now Max obviously intended to stake his claim. He unlocked the door, glanced at her again, then held up the key. His teeth shone in the shadows, his wolfish grin widening.

"Oh, no." Irish dusted her hands on her jeans and tugged down her Mickey Mouse T-shirt. Mickey's huge ears had settled exactly over her breasts like big signs pointing out the promising milk factories. "I don't have time to deal with you now, Mickey,'' she muttered. "Van Damme is squatting on my land, and he needs to be dealt with.''

"Move aside, will you, Irish?" Max ordered when she came to the doorway. He walked through the rooms and returned to her. Placing his hands in his back pockets, Max watched her closely. "Anger isn't good for the baby."

She held out her hand. "The key, Max. Then just pack up your—'' she glanced at the assortment of electronic doodads sticking out of boxes "—stuff, and mosey on down the road. You're not staying.''

"The hell I'm not,'' he said quietly, handing her a note. Max's hard jaw was covered with an evening beard and his hair was slightly rumpled. He looked very tough and determined. Not at all a likely daddy candidate. Or a gizmo guy.

Carefully unfolding the note, Irish read J.D.'s bold scrawl: "Irish. Max has just signed a year's lease for the cottage. If problems, call—J.D.''

"I'll call J.D.,'' she said, refolding and sticking the note in her jeans pocket. "What's the big favor you did for him?''

Max arched an eyebrow. The gesture made him look like a certified, very tough hit man. "I'll tell you someday when you're not wearing that frown. I intend to be a parent to our baby, Irish. Fight me, and I'll cause hell. There are such things as paternal rights.''

"You wouldn't dare, Van Damme,'' she began hotly, fiercely protecting the new life within her. Before she could move, Max's big hand slid out to gently grab Mickey's innocent face. Max tugged her near him, watched her for a heartbeat, then carefully, possessively placed his mouth over hers.

The long sweet kiss left her hungry and limp, melting against him. When his head lifted, his features had softened in the dim light. "I told you my biological urges hadn't been stirred, and now you'll have to suffer the consequences for opening the door. At my age, it's not likely that I'll get another chance at parenting, and I intend to enjoy every minute of our pregnancy."

The wolf's grin came and lingered. "I'm putting down roots, sweetheart," he murmured in a Humphrey Bogart imitation, his humor startling her.

While she tried unsuccessfully to counter his statement, Max kissed her again lightly. "I suggest you get used to having me around. By the time the baby comes, we should all be well acquainted. Don't worry, I'm going to be lovable and understanding. Right through the mood swings and the postpartum depression."

He punctuated the statement with a kiss that shattered Irish's last attempt to collect her thoughts. "There's no denying that you're carrying my child, Irish."

Max's lips roamed across her cheek to a spot that waited hungrily behind her ear. He kissed it lightly and she shivered in response. Unerring, the firm shape closed over her lips and she found herself answering helplessly....

A moment or a century later, he smoothed Mickey's ears back to their respective breasts and brushed her lips with his. "I've just realized that I've waited a lifetime for you and this baby. My biological clock and nesting urges are thoroughly stirred."

Four

"**D**addy," Irish repeated darkly the next morning when she entered the kitchen and watched Maxwell Van Damme swing fully into his new role. She'd overslept again, trying to escape the fact that Max had installed himself in Abagail's hideaway. When she felt up to it, she'd call J.D. and bribe him with the promise of cinnamon rolls, big fat ones with raisins and oozing with frosting. Max's roots needed transplanting.

Max was standing in her kitchen whipping up a frothy batter. Lined up in groupings of spices, grains and flours, just like toy soldiers ready for war games, the contents of her kitchen cabinets filled the countertop.

Granny sat on the back porch, rocking and muttering as she knitted. Her needles clicked frantically while the purple snake-thing growing from them slithered into a heap at her feet. Occasionally Granny looked through the screen to scowl at Max. Link sat with her, nodding frequently while reading his morning newspaper and sipping coffee.

Dressed in a "Bach Is Beautiful" T-shirt and worn denim jeans, Max padded comfortably around the kitchen in his stocking feet. He tossed a quick efficient smile at her over his shoulder. "I have everything under control," he said in his clipped businessman tone. "We're having raspberry crepes. Of course we don't have the framboise to flambé, but sifted confectioner's sugar will do. Don't worry, I've placed a special-delivery order with a Denver grocer. We're going to set up a computer link for orders later this morning. Like I said, everything is under control. All you have to do is rest for your doctor's appointment. By the way, we have an appointment with Denver's finest obstetrician at one o'clock. Katherine recommended him."

"My sister is in this...?" Irish floundered, trying words from plot to takeover.

Max slipped a spatula under the crepe and lifted an edge. "Damn it, Irish. An iron skillet just isn't a crepe pan. It's a wonder you've managed so far without one—or an omelet pan."

"*By the way,* you don't have me under control," Irish said quietly, firmly. A Maxwell Van Damme in her kitchen was something frightening. And Kat really had messed in the wrong lily pond this time! Irish frowned. Max with a lease wrapped in his fist confirmed that Katherine was out for revenge. A payback for playing matchmaker with her and J.D.

"Out, Max," she managed, suddenly ravenous for raspberry crepes.

"Mmm?" Studying the crepe clinically, Max slipped it on a plate and poured batter for another one into the pan. "Oh...can't. Sorry. I've signed a lease and there's this biological clock thing," he returned absently. "I couldn't possibly leave before the birth of my first child."

"I said," Irish enunciated slowly, distinctly, "that I wanted bran muffins, prunes and raspberry syrup over pancakes this morning—not wimpy pancakes."

Max turned to her as though he'd just remembered something. "Ah, of course. Stewed prunes for the traveler. I started marinating them last night with whole cloves and oranges. Irish, you don't have a decent set of measuring spoons or cups in the place."

"I serve them plain," Irish said, tapping her toe. Until now, no one, not even Granny had challenged her rights in the kitchen, and she didn't intend for a Van Damme to go tromping through her private territory. "I use scoops, pinches, ordinary spoons and coffee cups to measure, Max."

He nodded absently, then dipped into her rearranged refrigerator to extract a crock. Max emptied the spiced prunes into a cut-glass serving dish and inserted a proper spoon. He handed the prunes to a passing guest with instructions to place them on the breakfast buffet next to the orange soufflé omelet. Then he returned to making crepes, filling them with thickened raspberries, and rolling them neatly.

"So in keeping with the healthy inn picture," he said to Irish over his shoulder, "we present prunes every morning. By the way, Jeff's connection with the grocery delivery boy is amazing. Has to do with charging and splitting the fee for delivery.... I'll have to brush up on prune cookery. The house-brand-mineral-water idea is great."

"Not 'we'—me. I serve plain prunes, Max, available dried throughout the day and offered stewed in the morning," she insisted, willing to duel with wooden spoons if necessary to uphold her rights for serving plain prunes. "And stop throwing around accusations about Jeff. There wasn't a problem until you showed up."

Irish walked to the spice soldiers, took a deep breath and traced Max's alphabetical line up. "My most-used spices are placed forward and the least-used ones in the back," she said slowly as Max guided her over to the kitchen table. "This is *my* kitchen. You have to be certified as welcome to enter it."

"Uh-huh," he agreed absently, lifting her chin and inspecting her face clinically. He eased her into a chair with elaborate patience, making Irish's temperature rise. "You look better this morning."

"I'm not." Irish glanced at his discarded eggshells and stood. "We have guests who are watching their egg intake...."

"Ah, oatmeal, then," Max said, pivoting toward the canisters as though planning an attack.

"... and we use the eggshells for lime," Irish finished as Max selected a battered pan for heating water. He carefully measured four cups of water, covered the pan and measured two cups of oatmeal into a side bowl. The way he had leveled the cups of oatmeal by scraping a knife across the excess made Irish want to scream. Her kitchen had been invaded, violated, by a measuring fanatic, while she puttered along the merry taste-and-season route.

"Max, get the hell out of my kitchen," she said in a quiet yell as he began washing the eggshells. He dried and stacked them neatly in sets of four. Then he re-sorted the arrangement, placing the tops and bottoms together.

"Can't," he answered. "You're going to need a cook later and I'm getting the lay of the land, so to speak. The rest of your mob can't boil water."

"We'll try to manage without you. Why don't you just putt out of here in your little car?"

He stared at her, his hard mouth fighting a smile. "You mean the Porsche? Sorry, can't go. I never leave a job undone."

"I suppose my baby is *the job?*" Irish wanted to throw something, anything, at him.

"I started the whole event. Me. The father of the baby you're carrying. There's no reason for you to get upset about this, Irish."

Upset? she repeated mentally. The word was mild for the emotion she was experiencing.

After calmly ladling the thickened raspberry mixture into a crepe, Max rolled and sprinkled confectioner's sugar over it. When he had completed another tray of the crepes, he motioned a guest to add it to the buffet. Max poured the oatmeal into the boiling water, covered the pot with a lid and placed it on the cool rear burner.

Then he turned to her slowly. Slit at the neck to expose a small wedge of dark hair, the T-shirt added to Max's ultra-masculine kitchen image. The pastel flower pattern of the kitchen towel draped across his shoulder contrasted with his dark skin, a stark male beast bathed in posies. Unwillingly Irish took in the neat tight fit of his jeans.

Max, while not a lean man, didn't have an ounce of flab clinging to him. This morning, his body had a sturdy look to it, as though she could lean against him and wilt comfortably.

Lifting a thick brow, he looked down at her while he methodically dried his hands with the flowered towel. Finger by finger. Recognizing The Look—methodical and in charge—Irish groaned.

Then he hung the towel around his neck. "Irish," he said in his extremely patient tone, "last night I did a quick computer linkup with a medical library and scanned the library's banks on pregnancy. You're in the first trimester—three-month period—of pregnancy. You're easily upset, moody, and you may sleep more than normal. Last night you slept nine hours and fifteen minutes. Added to the nausea and the fact the situation isn't routine, you are also emotional. Nothing like the postpartum—after the birth—depression can be, but you need care."

"You scanned what?" Irish had always waltzed through the weeds in her daisy fields alone. Max had ventured to stick his crepes and omelets into her picket-fenced privacy. She grabbed a wire whisk stored in a pottery bowl and wondered about the penalty for kitchen abuse.

Max leaned his hips against the counter and crossed his arms over his chest. He shrugged, and the terry-cloth flowers seemed to curl lovingly around his strong neck. "I've never been a parent before and needed briefing. You need understanding and affection in this trimester, as in all of them." A muscle contracted in his jaw, and he lowered his brows. "If you need support, you're getting it. From me. I want to make it clear that any conferences with Riggs won't be acceptable from this point on."

"I can see who I want, Max. The baby hasn't anything to do with that."

"Boonie Riggs isn't playing father to my child," Max stated flatly. "I discussed the matter with him this morning. He understands. Make sure that you do."

"I understand that you're interfering with my life, Max," she threw at him. Despite her anger, the ruffled male image combined with the workman's clothing had strongly affected her. She wanted to throw herself into Max's arms and kiss away his grim expression. Irish remembered reading something about the possibility of a pregnant woman's increased sexuality. She groaned and closed her eyes, aware that Nadia had stolen a stuffed crepe and was making away with it.

"In keeping with your needs—until we can see a qualified doctor—were you sick this morning, and did you find the crackers and milk by your bed?" While Irish dealt with learning that Max had slipped into her bedroom and watched her sleep, he added, "I picked the flowers myself. I hope they meet with your approval."

His Italian loafers had been waltzing through her elegant rose bed, too. Van Damme's invasion had to be stopped. "I'm the flower picker around here, Max. Stay out of my beds."

He mocked her usage of beds with a lifted eyebrow, and Irish blushed.

Max ran his fingertips across her hot skin. "Fine. But you deserve someone else taking care of you. From the way things have been running—" Max emphasized the past tense "—it's easy to see that you do all the catering. From now on you save your strength." He held up his hand as Irish parted her lips to argue. "You should have fresh flowers beside your bed every morning. Just because you're pregnant with my child doesn't mean that you can't have all the little perks you deserve."

He glanced at Granny who was staring through the screen, then lowered his voice. "We want our baby's mother to feel loved and pampered, don't we?"

Before she could place Max, the kitchen beast, alongside Max, the father of her baby, he sat on a chair and eased her onto his lap, holding her stiffly and carefully. After a second in which Irish fought her need to be close to him and to thump him with the whisk, Max eased her head to his broad shoulder and placed his arms lightly around her. "There," he said, evidently proud of himself. "I am determined to coddle you, make you feel secure. What do you think?"

With her cheek riding the uneven rise and fall of his chest, and her body warmed and comforted by Max's larger safe one, Irish couldn't pinpoint any problems at the moment. "About what?"

Max smoothed her hair. He bent to speak quietly in her ear. "I'm not what you might prefer, Irish. But I intend to be a part of the pregnancy and, thereby, a part of your life."

"You have no obligation . . ." she began.

"What you need to know, Irish," Max continued, nuzzling her hair and holding her more tightly, "is that I'm rather awkward at showing affection. But our baby should experience affection now. Don't you agree?"

Max tensed and Granny turned her back to them. The lines beside his mouth deepened, and Irish found herself exploring them and his bottom lip. It appeared to be more touchable than his firm upper one.

Max kissed her fingertips before frowning and murmuring, "I couldn't find a really good reference in the computer for giving physical comfort to babies, in or out of the womb. But there has to be some sort of manual on it."

He paused, swallowed and took a deep breath as if to steady himself. "I'm forty-two, Irish. And I don't intend for my only child to lack anything. Right now I'd like to place my hand over our baby. May I?"

"Didn't anyone ever cuddle you, Max?" Irish asked. How lonely, she thought, grieving for Max as she moved his large warm hand to her abdomen. He should have some warmth, she decided as the lines on his face softened and the tension around his mouth eased.

"My pet boa constrictor tried," he returned, watching her expression with flickering dark eyes as he traced her flat stomach. The naughty-boy look fitted Max well, Irish decided when she realized he'd been teasing.

"Poor Max," Irish soothed, kissing the rough line of his jaw and running her palm across his chest. She ached for him, settling more comfortably into his lap.

Max stared down at her for a moment, then slid his hand beneath her cotton shirt, cupping one of her breasts. He trembled, gathering her nearer as he ran a thumb across the sensitive crest.

Irish breathed lightly. Against her throat, Max's rough face was heating, and she recognized the instant tenseness of his body. She inhaled sharply as his fingers edged beneath her bra, caressing her. "Oh, Max!" she breathed, aware of his hard body against hers and remembering the passion they'd shared.

"Hmm?" he asked, distracted by her other full breast. "My God, you're perfect, Irish—"

His hand stopped, and flushed Max leaned back to look at her closely. "That's right," he said, as if just remembering her pregnancy. "You're probably extremely tender, and here I am—" he broke off shakily, stunned by the sensuous moment.

Because she wanted to soothe him, Irish kissed his mouth lightly.

The kiss was meant to stay his fears, but somehow Max's mouth caressed hers gently. He lingered over her lips, brushing them and kissing the sensitive corners as his hand again settled gently over one bare breast.

"Max," she protested in a breath as he ran a possessive hand down her body. "Max, this won't do at all...."

"Mmm?" he asked, carefully fitting his palm over the new life within her. He watched his hand for a moment, then leaned his forehead against hers. His skin was slightly warm and clammy. When Irish tested the temperature of his cheek with the back of her hand, Max paled slightly and attempted a lopsided smile. "I'm just not used to the altitude yet. I'll get over it."

"Max, you are banned from my kitchen," she ordered as gently as she could while smoothing his damp brow. "I'll finish breakfast if you want," she said, sliding from his lap.

Max paled and placed a cold bottle of buttermilk against his cheek. "Ah...that's right. We're having raspberry crepes, aren't we?"

He closed his eyes, and Irish wondered if she'd really seen a shudder cross his wide shoulders. Or was it just the posies sliding over the terry cloth? Max patted the kitchen towel across his damp forehead. His dark face paled again when he glanced warily at the crepes. "Ah...maybe you could finish...just for this morning. I still have some layout plans to go over."

Walking quickly to the door, Max shuddered again and ordered, "Don't forget to enter what you had for breakfast in the notebook lying next to your handbag. Keeping track of the four food groups is important. This morning you can have a half cup of orange juice, a half cup of oatmeal with brown sugar and a cup of milk."

After Max's color returned, Irish allowed him to push her around. She realized he might be fragile, since his biological clock had just started ticking. Max seemed to send off good-natured laser beams, and she didn't have the heart to strip his new father mood from him. She even felt like patting his head when he began installing a computer system in a large closet. When he was gone, she'd close the door and nail it shut.

In the late morning, Irish snipped fresh chives from the herb garden and plotted to snip Max from her inn and her life. Along the way, it was necessary to show her big sister that she could manage her life. Irish had just placed the basket of freshly harvested herbs on the kitchen counter when Katherine called. "So what's new?" Katherine asked in the cool legal-smegal lawyer tone that Irish recognized immediately.

"Nothing," she answered cheerfully and listened to the heavy silence stretch from Denver. Irish swept a sprig of peppermint around her chin, sniffing it appreciatively.

"Nothing?" Katherine asked, and Irish smiled, feeling righteously wicked.

"Well, the Romaines are leaving today. I told you about them. You know, the young couple needing just a breath—"

"Irish!" Katherine demanded, the cool tone gone. "I want to know everything about you and Max, and I want to know now."

Sniffing the peppermint sprig again, Irish grinned. "Max? Max who?"

"Max, the father of your baby. Do you want me to come down there and pry it out of you? I can, you know. And while I'm at it, Max deserves to be cut down to size..." Katherine pushed.

"But J.D. told you to butt out, right?" Irish finished for her. Katherine's silence proved her theory right.

"J.D. has nothing to do with this. Max called me last night wanting to know the name of my obstetrician. I had no idea *you* were the expectant mother and *he* was the father—until he informed me that he was taking time off from his career to spend time with you and his child. Okay, I admit J.D. had a little to do with throwing Max at you, but Max did need to relax...er...ah..." Katherine struggled for the right phrase. "You do have a loving touch. Ah...Irish, I really think you should consider a paternity suit and support."

Irish stopped playing with the peppermint. "Kat, you and J.D. sent him here to devastate my management systems. You'll have to swallow the results and the way I deal with my problems. Your niece or nephew and I can get along just fine without Max's ...contributions or interference."

"Your management whats? Where is Max? If he's there, I want to talk with him," Katherine said hotly in her out-to-get-justice tone.

Irish took a deep steadying breath, placing her hand over her flat stomach. Max's excitement over the baby had surprised her. She hadn't realized the Armani-Porsche scientist-type could be stirred, nor that he was so cuddly, or so lonely. If she didn't have the feeling that he was such an orphan needing a home and a hug... "Max is leaving shortly. It's his nature to finish loose ends, otherwise he'll stew and fret and get ulcers. I know the detailer personality. I've let them putter around before—it's good therapy. Oozes out the stress and they go away satisfied. A guest who likes to do carpentry once remodeled the parlor after I'd just had it done. Max is installing a computer gizmo in the closet. I'll listen to his plans, keep him from disturbing the other guests, and then he's out of here."

"Max putters?" On the other end of the telephone line, Katherine was quiet. Irish waited. In the background, Dakota yelled and Travis called to his dog. But Katherine's silence continued. Finally she said, "Irish, Max doesn't have stress. He creates it. He's infallible and as deadly in purpose as J.D."

"I just talked with J.D. this morning about the lease. He thought Max needed the rest and quiet for therapy. J.D. is sweet," Irish tossed back.

"Max isn't."

When Irish replaced the phone, she found Max snooping through her basket of herbs. "Where's the sage?" he asked. Then, turning toward her, Max's gaze caught and lingered on her tattered floppy straw hat studded with fresh daisies.

Dressed in a business shirt and slacks, Max had returned to his computer-for-a-heart image—except for the sexy gleam in his eyes.

Irish stood still, feeling as if she were being absorbed into Max, as though he were taking her apart piece by piece and stuffing her inside him. Max stepped closer, and the scent of his newly bathed skin caused her to shiver. He'd smelled exactly that way the night they...

She blinked, trying to keep her bare feet on the linoleum squares when the rest of her body wanted to drift against his. In the distance, wind chimes tinkled and a calf bawled for its mother. Link's hammer tapped, and Irish's heart thudded quickly to the beat.

Max's long slow look flowed downward, touching on the yellow cotton sun top with tiny straps. He searched the crevice between her abundant and tender breasts. Beneath the fabric, her heart had decided to turn flip-flops.

She wasn't prepared for his lazy smile, nor the prowling finger running across the ruffled low-cut bodice. Her freckles seemed to dance and threatened to jump from her skin into the palm of Max's warm hand.

Max's gaze traveled farther downward, heating the small tanned expanse of her waist before moving on. Unable to move away, she forced herself to breathe. Her image of "poor Max" had changed to that of a hungry Rottweiler circling a tray of savory hors d'oeuvres and debating which morsel to taste first. And second.

He lingered on the denim fringe of her shorts, running the prowling finger down her breast and hooking it on the waistband. He tugged her toward him experimentally, and Irish resisted as Max took in her soft tanned thighs.

The finger hooked into her pocket and tugged twice. As he looked down at her, the gleam in his eyes caused her to shiver, her temperature rising.

Then he smiled—softly, sexily, intently. Tiny laugh lines appeared around his eyes, which were sending messages directly into her disturbed pregnant-woman hormones. Irish wondered distantly why she wasn't moving away. She wondered if Abagail had anything to do with the way Max affected her. Or was it the baby playing with her heart?

Max tugged again, looking very wicked and sexy and hungry.

"Max..." she heard herself protest breathlessly as Max's large hand spread across her lower hips. He fitted her against him intimately, and Irish trembled as Max nuzzled her cheek.

His other hand slid around her back, easing her full breasts against his chest, and Max breathed unevenly, his wistful sigh sweeping across her hot cheek. He stood still, holding her gently to him.

Against her ear, he whispered roughly, "Do you know I've never held a woman like this before?"

Irish wondered frantically why she couldn't force her feet to carry her body away. Max continued to hold her, his warm hands caressing her back. "This feels so good," he said unevenly. "You're so soft, Irish. You'll know exactly how to give our baby what he needs, won't you?"

"Max, we shouldn't be..." she managed after forcing a swallow down her dry throat.

"We could go upstairs and lie down," he offered in a low soft tone that made her skin heat and her freckles dance.

He nuzzled her temple, kissing it as his hand wandered up her spine to caress the taut back of her neck. "Irish, please. I'm experimenting in affection," he murmured huskily. "I'll need someone to practice on before the baby comes. You're the likely candidate. Just hold still. Or you could help by holding me," he suggested, his hands caressing her.

"Max," she returned in a whisper, forcing herself to stand still. It wasn't easy when her mother-to-be hormones were racing wildly and screaming that she hold on to him. "You're not a candidate for a daddy."

He smiled against her hot cheek. "I've already passed that test, remember? You really could cooperate better, Irish."

She shivered, trying to quiet her seething hormones. When she turned to protest, Max's mouth fitted tenderly over hers.

His kiss searched and warmed—a gentle brush of lips over hers, his breath entering her parted lips. Max nibbled on the corners of her mouth, then ran his tongue across her teeth. His hand supported the back of her head, adjusting her mouth to his as though he could taste her until eternity.

Her hat slipped, falling to the floor as the kiss deepened and heated.

When it was finished, Max looked into her drowsy eyes and smiled sexily. He patted her bottom, issued a frustrated male groan and murmured softly, "Wear something comfortable for the ride to Denver. We'll leave at ten forty-five. Allowing for two rest stops, we should be at the doctor's office at twelve fifty-five."

Still wrapped in the need to hold Max tightly, Irish looked at him blankly. "Denver?"

"Mmm." Max's dark sexy eyes stared down at her well-kissed mouth as if he'd like to enter a marathon kissing contest. "Your first doctor appointment?" he reminded her. Looping a curl around his little finger, Max turned it to the light and studied the glistening strands intently. "If we're lucky, my dark genes won't override your lighter ones. I'd love to have a little girl with gold-and-strawberry hair. And big sky-blue eyes."

He kissed her nose lightly. "I didn't get a chance to find out—do these freckles cover your entire body?" he asked huskily.

When she didn't answer, Max gently patted her bottom again. He grinned sheepishly when she glared at him. "I like this demonstrating-affection thing. The benefits are great."

"Don't get used to it, Max," she said fiercely, stepping away to calm her stressed hormones. "You won't be here long. A systems warrior isn't on my Santa Claus list."

Max's expression stilled, his grin replaced with a frown of determination. "Of course you see me that way—now. We're in this thing together, Irish. Remember, a pregnant woman needs attention. I'm going to give it to you."

"You shouldn't feel obligated," she began, startled by the raw savagery of Max's expression.

"Obligated? I'm not that noble." He paused, his flickering eyes pinned on her face. "You're delectable, Irish, pregnant with my child or not. If you think that my... honor has anything to do with my feelings for you as a desirable enchanting woman, you are one hundred percent offtrack."

"Max," she tried gently, "you're confusing the father role you feel obliged to play with how you feel about me."

"The hell I am," he stated low in his throat, anger swirling around him. "Try again."

She thought better of arguing when Max stepped nearer. She wanted him to hold her, she realized suddenly. Wanted him to kiss and soothe her. Badly frightened by the need to step back into Max's protective arms, Irish placed her hand over her tender lips and fled the room.

The remnants of Max's leashed anger seemed to cling to him like a dark swirling cape, despite his grim attempt to make light conversation on the way to Denver. Glancing periodically at his profile, Irish was uncertain how to soothe his ruffled Rottweiler image. Was it possible that expectant fathers needed care and affection, too?

Tormented by the thought that she had actually hurt Max, Irish allowed him to hold her hand. To ease his wounded pride, she might let him arrange an easy system for bookkeeping—before she sent him on his way.

She glanced down at his hand, laced with hers on her lap. Max's restless fingers rubbed her skin lightly, turned and fitted her palm against his. He toyed with the third finger of her left hand. "I've been married," he admitted cautiously. "Affection wasn't a part of that relationship. I want it to be a part of ours, Irish."

Unable to respond, Irish looked away. She'd given her heart away once, and now she needed to hoard it for the baby. Max glanced at her, his knuckles turning white as he gripped the steering wheel. He stared at the winding highway, the shadows of the pines slipping across his grim face.

In the doctor's parking lot, Max eased Irish out of the car with care. Just before entering the elegant building, Max paused and turned her to him, scanning her blue gingham cotton blouse and slacks. "You really look beautiful today...sweetheart."

While Irish dealt with the stiffly given endearment, Max guided her to the doctor's office.

Pacing restlessly and flipping through a magazine in the waiting room was Katherine MacLean. The elegant long-legged blonde glanced up when she saw them enter, her smoky eyes dark with fury. "Max, you should be ashamed of yourself," Katherine said tightly, furiously, then turned to her sister. "Irish, I don't know what to say."

"Say you're happy for me," Irish returned uneasily, sensing Max's tension. Katherine could be an imperial terror when tossing her big-sister image around, and suddenly Irish didn't want Max hurt. Tension ran through him like a live wire; she could feel it tingle in his fingers. She squeezed the hand that held hers. "Don't be afraid, Max. I'll protect you," she whispered in an aside to him.

Katherine glared at Max. "I want to see you in my office, Van Damme. Make an appointment. You're not walking away from this easily. I'll slap a paternity suit—"

"I'm not walking away from Irish," Max answered quietly, tightening his fingers around Irish's. "You checked Dr. Williams's calendar to see when her appointment was—I expected that much."

Katherine wasn't satisfied; she glanced at Irish, then glared again at Max. "Why Irish?"

"Because she's special," Max returned after a long moment as he searched Irish's expression. "I want her in my life."

"Yes, a baby would do that," Katherine said slowly, thoughtfully, after a moment. Her smoky eyes slid from Max's determined expression to Irish's face. "I had to see for myself."

Suddenly Katherine moved into Irish's waiting arms, and they hugged. "J.D. will be mad as a hornet that I threw my weight around, Irish. You'll calm him down, won't you?" Katherine whispered after a suspicious sniff. "Bake him something sweet and oozy. Put extra nuts on it. Have it special-delivered immediately—to his office."

Irish kissed her sister's damp cheek and whispered back, "Stay out of matchmaking technology, Kat. It takes a master's touch." Then she stepped back to find that Max had never released her hand.

He bent stiffly and kissed Katherine's other cheek. "I'll take good care of her."

Because Max looked so uncomfortable and Katherine needed a taste of humility, Irish grinned and demanded, "There, that was nice. You're doing fine, Max. Kat, you hug him and make up. His feelings bruise easily, and no matter what happens, don't hurt him. I won't have it."

Katherine's eyebrows shot upward. "You're protecting the deadly Maxwell Van Damme? The hit man you accused us of sending down to plague you?"

"Well—" Irish glanced at the nurse waiting for her "—he's that, too. But don't hurt Max, Kat. Hurry up and hug him, so I can go in. I won't budge until you do. Hug Max, Kat."

"Nobody ever hugs Max. Except Travis and Dakota." But Katherine grinned and hugged Max, who responded with a sheepish delighted grin. Somewhere at her feet lay her stiff resolve to boot Max out of Abagail's and her life. All the funny little hormonal disturbances were gleefully rioting, and she wanted a big dish of yogurt and olives.

After her preliminary examination and tests, Irish returned to the waiting room to find Max surrounded and chatting with three women. In varying stages of pregnancy, the women instructed Max on the role of father-to-be. Max nodded solemnly, asked questions, and took notes. In the corner of the room, a huge panda lorded over a realm of sacks and boxes bearing a toy-store logo.

Irish groaned silently, recognizing Max's absorbed expression and warned the women, "Don't give him any ideas. He has enough of his own."

"Wow. Is he yours?" a blonde in her ninth month asked wistfully.

Max smiled devastatingly. In fact, Max glowed. "Yes, I am," he said slowly. "Aren't I, honey?" Then he beamed as if he'd just mastered a new language. "Katherine had to leave for a court case. But she left me a list of be-good-to-my-baby-sister things. She thinks you need coddling."

"Oh, she does. Absolutely. Amen to that," the three women agreed in unison while Max intently shuffled through the bag of information booklets about pregnancy and childbirth.

Irish firmed her lips against her thoughts and pushed her lips into a tiny movement she hoped would pass for a smile.

Irish managed to stay calm as Max sat by her side during the doctor's instructions. Afterward, she was patient as Max packed the toys into the Porsche. "Katherine helped me pick them out in the store downstairs while you were with the nurse. She thought I was nervous, but she threatened me again—something about extended jail sentences and bread-and-water diets. But you'll protect me, won't you?" he asked smugly, sliding into the car.

Guiding the car into traffic, Max glanced at Irish. "You haven't said anything since the doctor's consultation. What's wrong? Don't worry, I'll be right with you all the way. I can't wait to begin the prepared-childbirth sessions. You could start exercising now—I like the idea of coaching my child into the world," he stated proudly.

Irish frowned, disliking Max's preening in the father role. She slid her hand from his and crossed her arms. "Max, *you* and the doctor had a consultation. *I* wasn't allowed to speak. Except to answer ways of childbirth and if I intended to breast-feed."

"Oh. Was there something he didn't answer? Are you having problems that we should know about?" Max was genuinely concerned, nudging the panda's furry paw from his ear. A yellow rubber duck worked its head out of his shirt pocket. "Irish, the first trimester is very dangerous. Katherine said your great-grandmother—who had wicked pansy-blue eyes, too—turned moody in the first stages of pregnancy, just like you."

"Me? Moody? Wicked eyes?" she asked, feeling distinctly prickly. "Max, everyone loves me. I'm adorable. There must be something wrong with you—"

"Irish, once we get through this stage—"

"Damn it, Max. Will you stop saying *we?*"

He shot her a long cool level look. "I'm in this, Irish." He placed his hand over her abdomen and caressed it briefly. "We're in this together. The three of us," he added, warmth returning to his dark eyes. "Just leave the details to me," he ordered mildly before Irish groaned, closed her eyes and slid lower in the luxurious seat.

Max took her limp hand. "That's right, dear. You need rest. Did you know that every woman in the waiting room was married? We might start considering..." he was saying just as she fell asleep.

In the next few days, Irish didn't have the energy to confront Max. But when she was feeling better, Maxwell Van

Damme would have to install his gizmos, new kitchen appliances, utensils and himself elsewhere.

If only he weren't so obviously satisfied. Glowingly content.

Delighted to have her under his thumb, Max puttered, ordered new gizmos and cooked for the guests. He'd taken over her specialties with delight, such as mixing the nightly egg-and-oatmeal face masks with crushed cucumber base and sitting in the kitchen with the female guests, drinking herbal tea. He straightened her rows of aloe-vera sprouts and devised a body wrap using the plant pulp. Max meticulously measured alfalfa seed and water in his sprouting jars and the results were perfect.

That grated. Before Max's interference, she'd been the champion alfalfa-sprout grower. She'd been the one passing out the facial masks and listening to troubled guests beneath the maple tree.

Somehow he found the time to pamper Irish, seeking her out from her hiding places and following Katherine's request for coddling. Irish didn't think she liked being coddled; her patience wore thin each time Max placed his arms around her and held her lightly. She was too busy dozing and wondering about when her breasts would stop inflating.

While she took naps, Max deposited bouquets, milk and crackers on her bedside table. He seemed to know instantly when she was nauseous, urging her to rest before he lay down beside her. "High-altitude problems," he would explain again weakly, holding her hand, "something I picked up in the Himalayas.... Where do you think we should put the nursery?"

In the hot afternoons, Max maneuvered Irish into elevating her legs by lying down and napping. In the rocking chair near her bed, he studied the doctor's pamphlets and splashed his thoughts about their combined genetic traits in his growing notebook. Then he managed to stretch out for a nap at her side, and sometimes, when she awoke...

Irish wanted to make love to him. She wanted the sweetness and the delight of having Max's gentle trembling hands moving over her.

Reluctantly she would force herself away, fighting the urge to dive on top of Max's delectable body. After all, she wasn't Mimi.

Five

————

"This time your man is building a helicopter pad, Irish," Jeff said, leaning against the laundry-room wall. He tossed a long roll of paper at her. "Check it out. Van Damme has plans for sticking an airport right in the middle of the north field. Looks like he's got plans for a hangar, too. What I want to know is, who's the boss around here? You or him?"

"Where did you get these?" Irish spread the blueprint over her folded bed sheets. At four months into her pregnancy, Irish had wilted under the August heat and the fact that she was losing control over her life.

She needed to call her parents about the baby. But what would she tell them about the father? She hated feeling like she'd trapped Max and that he felt obliged to blend into a rustic boring life-style. That he felt duty bound to put on a happy face when he could be systemizing Tahoe or Switzerland. Or discussing classical music with other highbrowed buffs instead of reading volumes on pregnancy and baby care.

On the other hand, Max's gentle rubbing hand was heavenly when the yogurt and olives decided to roll around uncomfortably in her stomach.

Irish forced a smile, remembering Jeff's presence. "Well? Where did you find the plans?"

He shifted restlessly. "I found 'em.... Van Damme has been all over this place with a fine-tooth comb. He's jumped me and my men once or twice, but I handled him. And I've turned in the bills to him just like you said."

Irish remembered Boonie's nose and wondered how Jeff had managed so easily. "How did you handle him?"

"Just told him that it wasn't good for you to get upset and that he was disturbing you plenty. Anybody can see that you're not as perky and happy as you were before him. Took the air right out of him."

"And he let it go at that?"

Fury leapt in Jeff's expression. "Hardly. He's a cool one. All business. Seems he's keeping a list on me. Let me know he respected your decisions about the running of the place. Told me to watch it and that he wanted 'any personal differences settled between us' away from you."

Irish scanned the blueprint, defining the plans and thinking of Max's noble efforts as the pleased father-to-be. He was protecting her, backing off from a situation that normally called for sharp Rottweiler teeth.

She frowned at the plans, thinking of Max's detailer personality. It must have cost him to avoid a confrontation with Jeff, who wouldn't disappear quietly.

Her own scene with Jeff wouldn't be pleasant. She didn't want her overstimulated emotions affecting a man who supported an elderly mother and disabled daughter. When she felt up to dealing with him, she would.

Despite the situation, a warm little leap of pleasure went through her. *Max respected her business decisions.*

Jeff continued, "He's got some idea that you'll handle things when you can. Says he's got confidence in you." His face twisted with anger. "We can do without him. He'll be on his way soon enough when he figures out that we're a penny-ante hotel."

"That's enough, Jeff," Irish said softly, glancing up at him while she rolled up the plans. Jeff had been needling her since Max's arrival, and she didn't like defending herself, nor Max. "Abagail's may be small, but we give our guests quality care. Remember that. And by the way, while you're working here, don't charge guests for minor car repairs or for any of the services they should have free. The Obersons didn't really have the fifty dollars you charged for chauffeuring them to the airport."

Jeff's mouth tightened, his eyes narrowing at her. "They're rich. They can afford it. Van Damme has you jumping through hoops. Anyone can see it. Before he came, you always let me do my job how I saw fit. No need to jump me because you're prickly, Irish."

She arched an eyebrow at him. Challenging males weren't her favorite animals this morning. "Make sure you get the field crews started on changing the sprinklers in the clover. We'll be harvesting the honey soon, and the clover flavor sells well. The carrots and tomatoes need more water...and the raspberries. Then check in with the Langtrees—they want to try out the horse-and-buggy moonlight ride this evening."

Irish continued to rap out orders, disliking her rising temper. "And by the way, don't ever call Max my 'man.'"

"You're having a baby by that—" Jeff glanced at Irish's flushed face, then clamped his lips closed. "Irish, Van Damme is nothing but trouble. He's interfering with the way I do business. He's asking for receipts and checking every penny. Wanting things 'itemized.'" Jeff's mouth curled distastefully around the word. "Don't like everything being changed. Whatever he's got going with you, he isn't my boss, is he?" Jeff demanded sullenly.

"He doesn't have anything going with me now." Irish faltered, thinking of the way Max's eyes tracked her. Like a wolf waiting for a lamb to weaken. Like a man eyeing a deliciously slim sexy beauty dressed in a tiny bikini.

Irish wasn't ready to deal with Jeff, but Max was another matter. She said goodbye to the sulking man and marched off to find Mr. Van Damme.

"Where's Max?" Irish demanded a few minutes later as she tapped Link's fishing newspaper with the roll of blueprints. The August heat had settled heavily on the inn, and the guests were nestled in their cool rooms, waiting for Max's promised Baked Alaska that evening. Max could bake the state of Alaska for all she cared, but he couldn't build helicopter pads at Abagail's.

Continuing to rock in the shade of the back porch, Link peered over the top of his newspaper, flicking an appreciative glance down Irish's loose peasant blouse and denim cutoffs. "See where the brown trout are biting over at Newman's Spring... Max is puttering at the barn. Now that he's got the solar-heating panels installed and adjusted for heating water inside, he's building an automatic gizmo to dispense Morticia's and the horses' grain. Looks like a good system—grain comes down the main chute, then goes into each stall when the animals need it..."

On a course set to destroy Max's latest plans, Irish absently returned six-year-old Patty Shoemaker's wave and toothless grin. She ignored the sweeping fields baking in the heat and the new Hereford calves playfully butting their heads together. Max had to be stopped.

She marched through the barn, nodding politely to Morticia as she passed. Following the sound of Max's hammer, Irish emerged on the back side of the barn. Shading her eyes against the early-afternoon sun, Irish spotted Max and his new project.

On a bale of hay was an empty yogurt carton and a can of black olives. Mimi lay on top of another bale, watching Max intently and twitching her tail. The barn cat was heavily pregnant and craved Max's attention, which he supplied by rubbing her tummy and sweet-talking her until she grinned and purred sumptuously. Irish frowned, regarding the cat as a traitor to her sex. The soothing strains of Bach swirled around the barn, and she remembered Max's statement that music was good for animals, too.

Irish swallowed, trying to ignore the sight of his tanned broad rippling back tapering down to the strip of pale flesh above his low-cut jeans. She didn't want her eyes strolling down his backside and long legs. But somehow they did anyway.

Fighting to keep her emotions in line, Irish tapped him on the shoulder with the roll of plans. "You blueprinting macho dictator. You low-down city list-maker."

Max placed the hammer aside and turned slowly toward her. A wild daisy was tucked behind his ear. He took the blueprints from her and placed them beside the hammer, then looked down his arrogant nose at her. "Is there a problem . . . sweetheart?" he asked coolly.

"Bingo! You've got it!" Irish fought studying the effect of fragile white petals against his darkly tanned skin. With new laughter lines radiating from his eyes, Max's face had taken on a lived-in quality. Irish fought the wave of sensuality washing over her. Her fourth month of pregnancy was not the time to discover how badly she wanted to dabble in Max's lovemaking. She shivered, trying to avoid remembering their first episode. If only she weren't in tune with Max's sexy new Western look; he had no right to be so devastatingly appealing. "Just what are you doing wearing a daisy?" she demanded.

"Nadia said I'd need it today—a good-luck charm. Cool down and tell me what's bothering you."

Cool down? Irish thought wildly. She didn't want the hot look in Max's eyes to set off tiny electrical charges and an instantaneous need deep in her body.

She didn't want to need Max, daisy behind his ear or not.

But Max's hand was tunneling beneath the weight of her hair to rub the back of her head. The gentle caress stilled her as effectively as his strong arms. Irish's body melded with his instantly, startling her. She wasn't prepared for the swift hunger racing through her, the stark desire written in Max's intent expression. Against hers, his body hardened, the denim jeans chafing against her bare legs.

While she managed to inhale, Max's dark eyes were skimming down her body, lingering on her full breasts. He lifted the heavy curls from her neck, allowing the breeze to cool her skin. He crushed the strands, watching her intently. A flush ran along his cheekbones, his expression darkly intent. "Do you have any idea of how much I want you?" Max asked through his teeth. His fingers edged up under her denim shorts, tugging at the elastic of her briefs. "Why the loving names?" he asked, sliding his fingertips along the rounded softness of her hips.

Irish's brain scrambled to remember the reason for her anger. Somehow Max had defused that anger, splintering her emotions into a devastating heat. "You're plotting to build a helicopter pad, Max."

A bee droned nearby, sashaying past them on its way to a field of clover, and Max eased her into a narrow slice of shade, concealing them from the inn. "Jeff's been snooping where he shouldn't be. He'll have to stop that. The pad is a practical idea, since Colorado is famous for snow-blocked roads in early February—your due date. A helicopter would be dependable transportation."

Max leaned against her, foraging for that sensitive spot behind her ear, and Irish's resolve to step free slithered away on the soft pine-scented breeze. "Max..."

"You are exciting, Irish," he whispered against her damp skin. "Do you have any idea how you can stir me?"

Of course she knew how Max had been stirred! She had been just as stirred! Irish closed her eyes, trying to lock her knees to keep them from giving way. Max's arm looped around her waist, scooping her to him just as he stepped backward and fell into the soft fragrant hay.

Lying on top of Max's aroused body, Irish trembled with the need to hold him. She didn't want to reach out and stroke his cheek, to savor the rough stubble chafing her palm. If only he didn't look so intent, so needing of her touch. Max needed to be stroke and loved, she thought dreamily, lightly kissing his lips.

She trailed kisses over his face, finding his cheekbones and pursuing them down to his mouth. Did Max have the same sensitive spot behind his ear? Would it ignite with her kiss? she wondered.

Beneath her, Max lay perfectly still. "God, Irish," he murmured quietly. "I thought I was past needing a woman like this."

Blueprinting scoundrel or not, Irish thought, Max could do marvelous things for her ego.

"Did I ever tell you how much I like your hips?" he asked huskily on cue, caressing said parts in a movement that brought her deeper into the cradle of his long legs.

"My hips?" Irish managed blankly, remembering all the hours of inch-reducing exercises she'd logged in with Mark.

"Mmm." Max's teeth tugged at the elastic bodice of the peasant blouse.

"Oh, my," Irish whispered as he found the tips of her breasts through her cotton bra. She wanted Max and it frightened her. "You're not stuck with me."

His head came up, his expression intent. "What if I want to be?" he asked softly, his thumb gently rubbing her inner elbow.

While her body wanted to respond, Irish fought to keep her thoughts stacked neatly, like Max's spices. "I understand your need to set up college funds and financial trust whatzits for the baby. And I understand why you're concerned that our baby have the best of care, the best diet, the happiest mommy-to-be. You're an honorable man, Max. But we're not anything alike. In fact you drive me batty.

But I don't want pity or honor to keep you here. And I don't want you acting as though..."

She couldn't meet the dark mocking humor in his eyes and looked away at a doe grazing in the meadow. "You don't need to pretend you really want me, Max."

Irish closed her eyes slowly, helplessly, when Max found that traitorous spot behind her ear. "You are so delectable," he whispered in a low rough tone.

"I'm not a roast-beef sandwich...." She ran out of breath as Max's hard body leaned over her.

"Mmm, with enticing hints of spicy mustard and horseradish."

After her freckles had been individually charted by Max's lips, they began walking back to the inn. With his slightly wilted daisy behind his ear, Max strolled beside her whistling *Bolero*. On the back porch, Irish tried not to crush the large bouquet of daisies that Max had picked for her.

Burying her face in the blooms, Irish hugged the thought that Max was the first man ever to pick flowers for her.

When she blushed and looked away into the zigzaggy peony fields, Max tipped her face to his and kissed her nose. He grinned rakishly. "I've traded the Porsche for a station wagon. It will arrive sometime tomorrow. After all, we'll need more room when you expand, won't we?"

Carrying her hand up to his lips, Max nibbled on the center. He smiled wickedly, smugly. "Will you marry me?"

Irish stared at him blankly, her emotions playing tug-of-war as they ran wildly through her. Her lips parted to say no, but her heart cheered yes, yes! and did joyous flip-flops.

While he waited, Max's confident male expression reached right inside her, and sensitive little chords all went *whang!* at the same time. Then Irish began to cry.

Because she was crying and didn't know why, she looked up helplessly at Max's taut, yet vulnerable expression. She sniffed, fighting the tears. "Don't look so frightened, Max. I...just...

want . . . to . . . cry. . . ."

"Look, Irish," Max began uncomfortably, shifting on his long legs. "Maybe I didn't pick the right time or the right way. . . ."

She looked up at him helplessly, the harsh angles of his face softened by her tears. "I can't . . . stop . . . crying. You haven't done anything wrong . . . but I just can't marry you today," she managed between sobs. "Lora Canfield is calling to let me know how much money the tooth fairy left under her pillow. . . . It's her front tooth and she's expecting the fairy to be generous."

Max ran his fingers through his hair and closed his eyes briefly. He looked like a swimmer caught in a crosscurrent, trying to find a safe bank on the shore. Irish tried for dignity and failed, the tears running down her cheeks. "Oh, Max, please take me to my room?"

Max muttered something ominous beneath his breath before he swept her up in his arms.

Beside them, Link rattled his newspaper. "Don't just stand there, boy. Take her to bed. Nadia can bring up the olives and blueberry yogurt."

"I hate crying," Irish managed weakly against the security of Max's strong shoulder. Because Max was so competent, so safe, Irish gave herself to his care. When she was better, she'd fight his takeover and convince him that he really didn't want to marry her.

Three weeks later, the strains of Rachmaninoff flowed around Max as he lay in the madam's opulent mirror-lined boudoir. Uncomfortable with the sensual need riding him, Max ran a hand across his bare chest, wishing Irish's inquisitive fingers were there in lieu of his. Dammit! He loved Irish's sunshiny smile, his name on her lips. But she was keeping him at arm's length.

Max slung his pillow at the wall. He'd slid away from relationships for years, and now when he wanted to wrap up Irish in legalities, she wasn't buying.

Maybe her loving instincts were right.

Maybe he wasn't worth taking the risk. The Van Damme dominant genes weren't affectionate ones. He shuddered slightly, remembering the way his father had shaken his hand when Max the child needed a hug.

Max studied the photograph Nadia had slipped him as a reward for letting her tell his future with tarot cards. Circling her, he'd endured Nadia's clucking and nodding; he'd discovered that Nadia wanted to write the story of her life from Romania, to New York, then to Kodiac. Forty-five minutes of crystal balls and cards had been a good investment, and at the end Nadia had rewarded him with a photograph of Irish.

Standing in front of a trellis dotted with crimson roses, Irish smiled back at him, sunlight dusting her hair with gold. In return for the photograph, he'd let Nadia use his computer in the cottage. Pecking away in his study, the fortune-teller was too busy to interfere with Max's plans for Irish.

Irish never turned away orphans, and Max counted on Nadia's presence in the cottage to support his homeless look.

He turned his head slightly to view the painting hanging above the fireplace mantel. Jonathan had captured Irish's loving sweet innocence perfectly in his soft Renoir style.

Jonathan was Irish's pet, Max thought darkly. But the artist fed upon his fears, turning to Irish for comfort. Max's fist tightened on the delicate crystal stem of his wineglass. Jonathan overcharged the guests for his landscapes and portraits, reveling in his starving-artist role.

Max scowled at the portrait of Irish, which had cost him enormously. He ran his hand across his flat abdomen, rubbing it tentatively. The muscles were taut, his skin seemed stretched over them. Max continued rubbing as he thought about plucking Irish from Jonathan's clutches. The young artist's pictures should be hung in galleries around the world and sold for top prices. But fear kept him clinging to Irish's soft secure nest.

Jonathan should be ripped from the inn and tossed into a den of hungry critics. Critics went for the jugular, and if he survived, they'd put a fine salable edge on Jonathan's talent.

After mentally dealing with Irish's beloved mob, Max had headed straight for Jeff. Jeff had been skimming major amounts from Irish's operation for years. At first the amounts had been small, but in the past year they'd soared to thousands of dollars.

Overpaid and lazy, the ranch manager had Irish's sympathy. According to Irish, Jeff mailed every paycheck to his elderly mother and disabled daughter. According to Max's investigation, Jeff didn't have a family, other than a girlfriend he liked to squire to Cancun. Several choice pieces of farming equipment were mysteriously missing, and Max suspected Jeff had profited from that.

Max ran a hand across his jaw. Jeff needed to be handled delicately and away from Irish's soft heart. Right now, she needed confidence, and exposing Jeff's activities could possibly harm her.

Trying to ease the tension in his body that thoughts of Irish aroused, Max lifted the decanter of fine wine next to his bed and poured more into his glass. He lifted the drink to toast the many mirrors reflecting his lonely bed, then emptied it. Pouring still another, Max thought of their baby. Babies needed love, not nannies and laboratories. Irish would be a perfect parent. But would he?

Irish's discomfort showed more every day. *How could he tell her about the guilt that plagued him?*

And how could he find the words to tell her of his unshakable fear that something might go wrong? He shuddered each time he thought of childbirth complications. With the baby due in early February, Irish's contractions might start when the snow had blocked the passes....

She'd filled the emptiness that had haunted him all his life by wrapping him in her warmth and care, and he wanted to protect and cherish her. Why couldn't he tell her how he felt?

At four and a half months into her term, Irish stood in front of her bedroom mirror studying the edges of her unsnapped jeans' waistband and hoarding the house's quiet.

The late-afternoon air had stilled, promising a storm later. The guests were off on the annual September trail ride and would camp that night in a neighbor's huge barn. Granny and Link were spoiling their latest great-grandchild in Denver, and Nadia had locked herself in the cottage, writing frantically. Jonathan had suddenly received an offer to present his paintings at a art gallery and had left within two days. Max knew everything about shipping paintings and had helped extensively with the arrangements.

Jeff, scowling and snarling, had taken two days off to recover from Irish's recent discovery. The manager had chosen cheap paint for Abagail's siding, and after a month, it had begun to peel. He'd blamed the vendor, but when Irish called the store she'd learned that Jeff's order had been filled properly.

Irish tugged on her waistband, frowning as she thought of Jeff. A veteran with a steel pin in his hip and a plate in his head, he wouldn't find employment easily. As the only supporter of his elderly mother and handicapped daughter, Jeff needed understanding. Not the harsh treatment Max had suggested—an embezzling charge wouldn't help Jeff's dependents.

Accommodating Nadia's need for privacy during her final draft, Max had moved into a vacant room for a few nights—one he was considering for the nursery—and locked himself away in his closet-computer room to itemize, vandalize, and systemize.

The baby's kick startled Irish and she placed her hand against her side, awed by the tiny life within her.

The first time it had happened, she'd caught her breath and looked helplessly at Max who had immediately rushed to her. "What's wrong, Irish?" he'd demanded urgently, his expression taut.

"The baby just moved," she'd whispered helplessly just as Max picked her up in his arms, carrying her to the stairs.

He'd stopped in midstride, stared at the steps and had swallowed slowly. "Moved?"

She'd nodded and smiled, watching him slowly absorb the wonder with her.

"Our baby moved," he'd repeated, placing her to her feet. His hand had caressed her abdomen gently as he'd begun to grin widely. The next few days, Max had explored the tiny life almost hourly until he was rewarded by a movement. Tears had come to his eyes although he'd turned away.

But Max's scrutiny wasn't always welcome, Irish decided firmly.

She frowned and ran her palm across her abdomen. "You'd just better not be as methodical as your father," she informed the baby, patting her tummy. "I've had enough measuring, weighing, dieting and diagrams on how your growth is progressing to last a long long time. I'm fed up with genetic charts and chromosomes. Searching out the best hospitals for maternity care isn't my idea of a fun time."

She listened to the mellow chords of Bach winding up the dumbwaiter chute Max had just installed. "I could live without classical music, and the first word you say better not be computer," she warned.

The freshly baked aroma of Max's morning croissants mingled with Abagail's lavender scents. "Max might be under stress caused by his feelings of honor and obligation, but I could live without a resident chef."

But could she live without Max?

Irish shook her head and eased a length of clothesline through her jeans' belt loops. Tugging on a large T-shirt, she studied the effect in the mirror.

She'd been too busy fighting Max's menus and plans for the baby to notice the way she had changed. Her hair had grown longer, framing her face in ringlets as bright as the aspen leaves. Surrounded by the shining mass, her face was fuller.

There was something softer moving in her. It touched her mouth and deepened the color of her eyes. It was as though she had a wonderful secret and was hugging it to herself. Irish ran a finger across her bottom lip, testing the sensual contours. Of course, any woman's lips would seem sensual with Max exploring them frequently. Max seemed to love to taste her.

Irish studied the mirror. Thoughts of Max made her blush; the reflection's eyes shone warmly back at her. Wrapped happily in his father-to-be role, Max created lists of appropriate baby names on his closet computer. He installed an intercom in the nursery—once the madam's immense closet—and tested the sound system piped into the tiny room with classical tapes. Max's Himalayan nausea had eased. His drowsiness due to an old ear infection—also triggered by Colorado's high altitude and chill in the early fall breeze—had stopped.

A quick one-two knock on her bedroom door signaled Max's arrival. She jumped, feeling guilty that she had been thinking about the culprit. "Honey?" he said in a low intimate tone that caused her skin to tingle and her full breasts to harden.

Irish glanced down at the twin nubs thrusting against the faded cotton T-shirt. "Traitors."

She glared at the door that had caused everything. If she hadn't been fending off Boonie's advances by holding on to the crystal knob, Max's measuring spoons and cups wouldn't be in her kitchen. Max's protective streak would never have surfaced. . . . "Go away, Max."

"Amore," Max murmured beyond the door, and Irish winced. He'd been snatching Granny's romantic paperback novels and experimenting with endearments. Every time he tried a new foreign version, Irish's whole body went limp. Except her inflated sensitized breasts.

Irish threw up her hands, then opened the door slowly. Leaning against the wall and holding a cardboard box in his arms, Max stood looking down at her. "Hi, beautiful."

Longer and riffled by the autumn wind, Max's hair softened his face. The sun had lightened the auburn color; the new length waved deeply and rummaged down the back of his tanned neck. A skiff of curls played at the collar of his faded pink shirt. He'd just showered, and tiny beads of water clung to his hair and chest.

Hanging loosely down his stomach, the shirt was unbuttoned, exposing an exciting wedge of dark hair covering his chest. Irish fought the urge to nuzzle that gleaming curling wedge by gripping the crystal knob with trembling fingers.

His jeans dipped low on his hips and fitted snugly down the length of his legs.

Max grinned, a flash of white teeth in a darkly tanned face, and Irish's baby kicked her again in response. Unable to look away from his sparkling brown eyes, Irish placed her hand on her side, quieting the quarterback's running legs.

Max kissed her forehead. "Are you feeling all right?"

The movement presented her nose with an enticing whiff of newly showered male body and tangy after-shave. Irish closed her eyes against the impulses tugging at her to press her nose into his gleaming damp hair.

"It's my private time to relate to the baby, remember?"

Max straightened from the door frame and padded into the room. He dropped the contents of the box—an exercise mat, books and his white boxer shorts—on her bed. Then he drew a plastic tube from his back pocket and tossed it onto the bed. "We need to start working together, Irish. Exercising now will help us later."

Picking up the tube of cocoa butter, Irish leveled a stare at him. "What's this?"

"To aid skin elasticity." He glanced at her abdomen. "On our next checkup, we need to shop for maternity clothes. Or we could order a personal showing...."

His eyes lingered on her burgeoning breasts and he added softly, "You might want to try the cocoa butter—"

Irish held up her hand, pointing to the door. "Enough. Out. I'm having a conference with my baby. My...chest is my business and the baby's."

"What about exercising? You need to tone up your back, Irish. Preparing for childbirth is necessary and you are approaching your fifth month—"

"I'm not flabby, Max. Besides I've been exercising."

His eyebrows went up. "Did I say you were flabby? Irish, if we're going to work together, you've got stop being so touchy."

His eyes lingered on her endowed chest, and the reoccurring nubs responded happily. When Irish blushed, Max relented and tossed the boxer shorts to her. "Here, these will do for now. Put them on."

Irish placed her hand against her hip. Max's eyes had that challenging twinkle, his mouth curving with sensuous expectancy. She tilted her head, eyeing his lazy stance. "Max, I really don't like the feeling that I'm being hunted or pushed. Just because you feel you need to stick around and take care of me..."

His hand caressed her cheek, and Max moved nearer, leaning down to nuzzle her throat. "You'll have to start learning about accepting someone else's care, Irish. Namely my TLC. By the way, Katherine is concerned. Your parents haven't been informed of becoming grandparents again. Don't you think it's about time—"

Irish jumped back, rubbing the spot his lips had found. She glared up at him. "You stop that."

"Start exercising with me and I will," Max threw back smugly, flicking a glance at the books on her bed. "Then we can pick out names over my chicken Kiev. What about Shawnee or Sasha? Then there's Abagail, Tyree, Sloan, Sam..."

Irish lifted her chin, sensitive to Max's probing gaze, which always returned to her chest. But then again, how could he miss it? "I'm not into games today, Max. Torment somebody else. You have parents—go explain fifty-to-one odds to them."

When she mentioned his parents, Max's face stilled. He leveled a stare at her and said quietly, "This is not their concern."

Beyond the window, lightning lit the clouds racing across the sky, and Max frowned immediately. His gaze traced the dark clouds over the Rockies, and his face hardened. "I hate lightning," he said in a low tone. "In Missouri, thunderstorms can be hell for a kid."

A gust of autumn wind slid into the room, and his head went back as though taking a blow. Irish touched his cheek, smoothing the taut muscle there. Instantly Max caught her hand, bringing it to his mouth. He closed his eyes and she felt him searching his thoughts. "Max?"

When his lids opened, the fear and desperation in his eyes made her ache. He swallowed the raw emotion beating at him, his shoulders tense as he watched her warily. Whatever had caught him in its midst had made him vulnerable, and Irish had a glimpse of his internal scars. Max's pain needed tending and she instinctively reached out to him.

Looking fiercely alone, ravaged by something she couldn't fathom, Max picked her up and carried her to the bed.

Six

Held aloft in Max's strong arms, Irish absorbed the tension flowing through his taut body. The air crackled with the emotion driving him, as though the faraway lightning had splintered into the room. Thunder rolled in the distance, and Max's heart pounded beneath her palm. Framed by the window, his face was outlined against the gray clouds skimming across the late-afternoon sky. The breeze riffled his hair, and each time lightning shot silver fingers across the gray sky, Max's arms tightened around her.

Another stroke of lightning etched Max's harsh face against the shadows of the room. His loneliness reached out to her. She felt his ragged breathing, as his fingers pressed almost painfully into her.

His eyes were wary as her hand moved slowly around his face. She traced the hard jaw, the slashing cheekbones and the firm set of his lips. Beneath her touch, something desperate and vulnerable shifted, seeking her. Then it scurried away, shielded from her as Max looked out at the storm.

She'd had a piece of him then, touched it and cradled it in the palm of her hand.

"Max," she murmured softly, caressing his shoulder with her other hand. She felt his muscles ripple and shift. "What is it, Max?" she said, trailing her fingertip across his lashes. His eyes closed as if drawing the moment and her presence into him, and he breathed sharply.

"Sweetheart," Irish murmured, placing her lips lightly against the grim line of his mouth. Her fingers soothed the tense muscle in his cheek and came away damp. Was it the mist of rain, or was it the sweat of fear?

"This is the wrong time, Irish," Max warned when her lips slid along his cheek. "Control isn't something that I've got to spare right now."

"Sweetheart," she persisted in a whisper, knowing she was pushing him to the edge.

"No one has ever called me that," he murmured shakily, emotion darkening his eyes.

Whatever bound Max to the savagery of the storm, she would fight it with him. Unbuttoning his shirt and caressing his hard chest, Irish wanted nothing between them now.

Beyond the inn, the wind tore against the corners of Abagail's and bent the trees in its path. Lightning sent out silvery fingers to dance along the starkly outlined Rockies. Rain moistened her cheek as Irish wrapped her arms around Max's shoulders and held him tightly. "Come to me," she murmured against the rapidly pounding vein running down his throat.

"Irish, I'm warning you. This isn't the time for discovery games," Max said against the strand of silken hair tantalizing his skin.

But his arms had tightened around her—as if he'd never let her go.

She kissed the hard line of his chin lightly. "You're going to tell me about it later, aren't you, Max? But right now I want everything you want."

"What I want..." he said urgently. "Oh, damn..." Max shuddered, easing her to the bed. His hand slid down her arm to find her wrist, linking her to him. The gesture symbolized the new life within her and the strong bond between them. Irish wanted that—the knowledge that Max would fight to stay in her life. Max wasn't the type to run away in hard times.

He'd caught her hair, sending his fingers through the heavy mass and crushing the curls. Passion ran across his taut expression as he lifted her face to his.

Meeting his searching stare, she wanted him to know that she could match anything he could throw at her, the good or the bad. And when he was ready, they'd walk through the scars tormenting him together.

"Now, Max," she said as cool mist blew into the room, riffling the curtains. Taking her time, Irish slid her T-shirt up and over her head, then dropped it to the floor.

Max's gaze fell to her shoulders, flowing down her body to the baby. "Irish," he murmured huskily. "The baby. This isn't the time, Irish. You don't know what you're asking of me," he finished roughly.

She undressed slowly, and Max's face darkened with heat, his eyes following her movements.

Early-evening shadows slipped intimately toward them. Then distant thunder skimmed into the room. Max stiffened, shuddering; something hot and fearful raced across his expression, a desperation reaching out to her. Aching for him, needing him, Irish linked her fingers with his.

"Don't think about anything but now, Max," she whispered, looking up at him.

"Only now," he repeated, searching her eyes as she loosened his clothing.

The next time the lightning sliced across the Rockies, Max lay on the sheets with Irish.

His mouth ran hungrily down her, and she lifted her body to his lips, answering the mood driving him. When he returned to her mouth, Irish parted her lips for him, and wrapped him tightly in her arms.

Max moved swiftly over her, his mouth hungry and demanding. She answered his demands, taking him deeper. His urgency became hers, the hunger and the stark passion racing over through them with the intensity of the storm raging outside.

He wasn't tender; she hadn't expected anything but honesty.

Where she led, he followed. When he demanded, she gave. Tangled with the past, new passions and new discoveries soared between them.

Turning, blending, angles, softness, heat. Irish gave Max her pride, her past.

He took her into his pain, his desperation, his need to be consumed by her.

Riding the stormy passion, Irish held him tightly, absorbed him into what she was, what they could be....

Max's desperation spread through her and became her own. The eloquent pleasure sharpened, coming quickly now, and Irish placed her trust in Max to carry her safely through the stark passage.

At the crest of the flight, he waited for her. Then as she found him in that special place, Max gave everything, crying out her name softly. Spiraling over the silken edge, Irish paused in the strength and the glory, fought to linger in the joy they'd found, and heard Max's distant voice unevenly repeating her name as she dissolved into tiny quivering pieces.

Max found her mouth, kissing her and whispering to her. Over the sounds of the wind sweeping through the pine trees outside, the sweet urgent words were indistinct, yet comforting. Irish lazily returned the light kisses, running her palms down Max's broad back. She tried to open her eyes and couldn't. She wanted to remain where she was, warm and snug under heavy, dependable, huggable Max.

Keeping her with him, Max shifted slightly to draw a sheet across them. With an enormous effort, Irish tugged it up around his shoulders. She smiled drowsily at this new Max, this part-of-her-body Max. He'd given her a part of himself in the savagery of their lovemaking, some treasure she had yet to explore. With his hair mussed by her fingers and his eyes shining softly down at her, Max was cuddly.

Against the window, the rain fell softly, skipping into the room on the light breeze. Wrapped in warmth and wallowing in a pleasure she'd never experienced before, Irish wanted to keep Max with her.

Smiling wickedly back at him, she stroked the cooled contours of his shoulders and traced the cords running down his arms. Max did such wonderful things for her ego. "Maxi. Sweetheart. Sugar pie," she murmured against his mouth, teasing him.

Max's kisses had changed from sweet and lingering ones, to careless lighthearted ones that tasted of new passion. "Passion pie," he returned, and she felt his grin against her shoulder.

"Ah . . . Max?" she asked as his kisses trailed upward.

"Mmm?" Max found the spot behind her ear, and another round of fluttery little quivers shot excitedly through her.

"Max . . . the spot," she managed in a gasp as his tongue took up the search and his hands slid downward to cup her hips. Irish tested the spot behind Max's ear and he tensed.

"Again?" Irish asked, moving with him into the heat.

"This time we'll take it slow," Max said against her throat.

Later, Max tucked her against his side and they watched the lightning shimmering in the distance, its power spent and slithering away into the soft rainy night.

He held her hand on his chest and breathed quietly. "No one has ever seen me like that, Irish. Not since I was a child.

My parents couldn't bear that their perfect child, the product of perfect genes, was terrified of storms."

Then she understood. "So you fought the storms alone."

"Crying and huddling away from the sounds. When I was eight, the housekeeper said I disturbed her favorite program and she locked me in a closet for the duration." Max turned his head on the pillow to stare fiercely down at her. "I don't ever want our baby to be alone and afraid," he whispered urgently.

"He won't be, Max," she soothed.

"What if I can't give him the love he needs, Irish?" he asked rawly, the pain shimmering in his eyes. "My parents were just my age when I was born. They'd already formed their life before I arrived. In a clan of genetic doctors, I was the only child. Apparently, I was an experiment that my aunts and uncles hadn't wanted to try. The Van Damme family trait doesn't lean to hugs and kisses. Children can sense when a parent doesn't care. They feel... I don't want my parents coming close to you or our baby."

Sharing his pain, Irish smoothed a curling strand of hair from Max's temple and traced a heavily beating vein in his throat. "Later, when you were old enough, did you tell them how you felt?"

Max tensed, his eyes fierce. "I was too busy trying not to disappoint them, excelling in private schools."

"You could ask them here and—"

"No." His statement was flat. "They're not involved in my life. Especially now."

He paused, then softened the harsh statement as he added, "You have a loving heart, Irish. But you don't understand my parents. Don't ask me to invite them into our relationship or the baby's life. I want them away from here and you. I'll deal with them—by myself, away from here."

Irish placed her fingertips over his mouth and snuggled close to his warmth. "Shh. Don't worry, Max. Everything will be fine. Our baby will have everything he needs...." She hesitated, startled by the quick kick against her side.

"He kicked me," Max murmured, reverent pride threading through his deep uneven voice. Spreading his hand over the spot, Max waited and was rewarded by another delicate kick. "Hello, baby. I'm waiting for you," he whispered softly.

"Daddy," Irish murmured, watching his eyes light with pleasure and a grin slash across the shadows of his face.

Max rested his chin on her head, and she was comforted by the rise and fall of his chest. He continued to look out into the dying storm, searching out the lightning dying in the mountains.

"Call them, Max," Irish insisted softly, smoothing his frown with her fingertips. "Or go see them. They should know—"

"Let it go, Irish," Max ordered curtly. "They're not a part of this."

To let him sort out his thoughts, Irish remained silent and waited.

After a long while, Max turned his face from the window to her. "I'm staying the night," he murmured against her lips. "Tomorrow I'd better move back to the cottage while I can."

Snuggling back against Max's warm chest as she dozed, Irish thought she heard him murmur, "I never liked being an only child. We've got time to go for two...."

A few days later, Irish and Katherine watched Max repaper the nursery wall.

"Max is such a sweetie," Katherine said. "He's designed the traffic-flow pattern of the nursery, and he's refinishing Grandma's favorite rocking chair. And he cooks, too. What else could you ask for, baby sister?"

"He's a prince," Irish returned darkly, her gaze skimming the baby's toys and returning to Max. Dressed in tattered jeans and a flannel shirt, he looked delicious. As if he'd been waiting for her to wrestle him to the floor, roll him under the crib and have her way with him. "See if you like him checking ounces and calories on your dinner plate. Kat, I'm not used to being cuddled and tucked under anyone's wing—Max can be pretty overpowering."

"I know. You like to do the tucking. Maybe you should learn to accept someone else doing it for you. Sharing isn't an easy lesson to learn—I had to work very hard at opening up to J.D. You've escaped the tyrannies of a well-meaning spouse long enough, my dear little sister. Don't tell me you're deprived of the essentials. Max is taking good care of you. I saw him slip you that second helping of olives and yogurt. And this morning when he thought J.D. and I weren't watching, he burned and peppered your eggs just the way you like them. Max is spoiling you and you know it."

"He's just feeling obligated," Irish returned, catching Max's intimate glance at her. "The burned eggs are just payment for what he feels is a debt."

"Ah, that's why he can't keep his eyes off you. Of course. That's why he keeps touching and hugging and kissing you."

Irish blushed and looked away. "He's read about bonding with the baby. Right now, he has to deal with me."

Katherine laughed, running her hand down Irish's hot cheek. "Give up. The man's got a thing for you. Your franchise on loving has been sliced to ribbons. J.D. said that Max has laid out a flowchart for your lives, and according to it, you could be expecting again in two years. He's started hunting likely churches for a full-scale wedding—"

"Expecting again?" Irish ignored Katherine's giggle, moving past her into the cheerful nursery. Max's takeovers had to stop. Nothing had been on an even keel since he broke the fifty-to-one odds barrier.

Holding aside a strip of wallpaper decorated with tiny smiling bears, Max dipped to kiss her nose. "You were right. The teddy bears with the pink ribbons are really better than the ducks and the cats—"

"Don't patronize me, Max. Kat said you're planning another baby—" Irish stopped in midsentence, watching Max blush. The red coloring moving beneath his dark skin caught her broadside. "You can't have your way all the time," she finished limply.

"I'm late realizing my goals in life, dear heart. My biological clock just needed you to wind it up," Max said with a sheepish grin. "A second baby would be just perfect. After we're married, we could adopt—"

"Now, Max," Irish interrupted earnestly, feeling as though she'd been pushed into the number-one priority slot in a series of takeovers. "You're running a little fast here, don't you think?"

Max patted Irish's abdomen proudly. "We started out that way, but everything is in sync now."

"Marriage," she repeated carefully, trying to herd the king of the teddy bears back onto the current subject. "Max, as far as I know *we* have no plans for marriage and none for a second baby. Right now coping with you is enough."

"I know," he returned smugly. "But you do it so nicely."

His dark eyes shaded with a gee-isn't-this-great look, and Irish found her anger sliding out the open window.

Max kissed her on the nose. "My studies show that healthy reproduction at our ages is a possibility we shouldn't overlook."

Irish stared at Max's wide grin and wondered if she had heartburn, or if her heart had just caught another Cupid's arrow. Just then Max frowned. "What's wrong, Max?"

"Uh. Nothing is wrong. Must have been too much spice in the manicotti sauce at lunch."

In the background, J.D. chuckled and Katherine giggled. Dakota ran into the room, throwing herself into Max's arms. When he picked her up for a kiss, Dakota beamed. "Uncle Max says that Aunt Irish is gonna have a baby with black hair just like mine. He says Travis and me can baby-sit while he's out—'' Dakota struggled with the word, then grinned as she found it ''—dating Aunt Irish.''

Irish stared over the little girl's shining black curls to Max's haunted eyes. ''Dating me?'' she asked huskily. ''Why?''

''Figure it out,'' Max murmured, bending to brush her lips with his.

''She's five months along,'' Max told the nurse at the hospital's main desk. ''Dr. Williams has set up a tour for us.''

The nurse's sharp gray eyes peered over the top of her glasses to Irish. ''Yes, Dr. Williams said that since he lived within an hour of Kodiac, you might want this hospital rather than Denver's. With Mrs. Dalton's due date in February, this hospital would be the better choice and she can start having her checkups here at the doctor's rural clinic. We may be small, but we have all the necessary equipment and a very good staff. Mrs. Dalton will have the best of care.''

At Irish's waist, Max's fingers tightened slightly. His Rottweiler look had returned. ''We're not married.''

The nurse's white eyebrows shot up, her gaze shooting over Irish's loose yellow overblouse and black harem pants. ''Oh, I see. Then we'll proceed on the basis that Ms. Dalton's wishes alone will be considered. You realize that she can demand that you be barred from the birthing room.''

''In a pig's . . .''

The nurse pulled her lips back from her teeth, daring him. She'd obviously backed down bigger men, standing tiny and pristine in her white uniform and noiseless shoes. ''Yes, Mr. . . . ?''

''Van Damme. I'm the baby's father. And I will be at *Ms.* Dalton's side when she gives birth to *our* baby.''

''Hmm, we'll see. Dr. Williams wanted me to arrange the tour for several couples due at the same time, and they're waiting for you in the family room. Shall we go?'' she asked, swishing silently ahead of Irish and Max.

Taking Irish's hand, Max muttered between his teeth, ''I could tell her where to go.''

''Max, be nice,'' Irish urged. ''She won't invite us to the Pickles and Peanut Butter tea later. You'll blow your chance to meet the other fathers.''

''She's a bully,'' he muttered in an aside as the nurse looked back at them. But he smiled at the nurse; a disarming devastating male grin that most women returned without hesitating.

Unmoved by Max's attempt to make nurse points, she peered at him over her glasses. ''Five couples are taking the tour and attending the Pickles and Peanut Butter party later. Two months from now, you'll probably all be taking Lamaze classes from me. No chatting during the tour, except for questions. You can visit freely at the party.''

When they entered the room filled with couples of assorted ages, Max stopped midstride and stared at the other women. He gripped Irish's hand tightly. ''I don't like this,'' he stated ominously as though they'd just entered a den of man-eating tigers. He scouted the room carefully, his click-click-I'm-computing expression intent. ''They're all wearing wedding rings,'' he noted, the quiet statement dropping into the silence of the room. ''You're the only one who isn't wearing maternity clothes, and the only one who isn't married.''

At his side, the nurse smiled quickly and warmly at Irish. Then she looked up at Max's guard-dog expression. ''Dr. Williams told me that you were a tough commando in our overseas troops. Remember, Mr. Van Damme, that those techniques have a time and place. Cooper General Hospital is my turf,'' she said, then smiled. ''I think we'll all get along if you remember that, don't you?''

Max held Irish's wrist throughout the tour as though she might escape him. In the birthing room, his fingers trembled on her skin. In the delivery room, Max paled when the nurse described cesarean sections. When they came to the nursery with six babies wrapped tightly in flannel blankets and in rolling cribs, Max began to perspire.

He leaned his forehead against the nursery's glass window and closed his eyes, explaining that his stomach was just a little upset. The nurse patted him on the shoulder briskly and grinned. "I haven't lost a father yet, big guy." Then she plopped a Lamaze booklet in his hand and ordered, "Better study up. I'm the instructor, and when I say hop, you hop, mister."

Irish treasured the thought that Max could be bullied.

While Irish stood on a low ladder to wash the inn's windows, she thought about Max's fierce scowl down at the tiny nurse and grinned.

"Oh, no, you're not," Max said in the vicinity of her chest. Lately everything seemed to happen around her chest, including food crumbs that honed in on the generous shelf her breasts provided.

Max tugged on her loose flannel shirt gently. "Get down now," he ordered in a tone that stirred Irish's unsteady nerves.

"I'm quite happy here, minding my business. But thank you," she returned, ignoring him and squirting cleanser on the glass.

"Are we in a perverse mood today, dear heart?" Max asked. Lifting her into his arms, Max held her lightly. "You're not climbing anything but stairs."

"It's October, Max. Window-washing time. We can't get help, Granny can't do it, and you're working on gizmos—"

"Those are computer linkups to the stock market. Granny is foraging through the morning report right now. She and Link have just discovered the bull and bear markets and have invested in pork bellies. Where is Jeff's cleaning crew? They can handle windows, and if they can't, I will. They need caulking, too."

"You're a bully," she tossed at him, shaking with anger. "Barging in here, getting everybody to wait on me hand and foot...." Max was either too understanding and sweet, or demanding and arrogant, when she did something he considered taboo for pregnant mothers. The combination was upsetting. Lately, Max had been backing off from her brief but undeniable temper. It wasn't that she was moody with hormones swishing up one side and then the other. It wasn't that she'd toss at night, wishing for Max's arms to hold her. And she didn't like greeting the morning with a groan.

Irish frowned. Things just weren't perking along her way, and it was Max's fault.

She'd asked Jeff to paint Abagail's front porch for the group of "spit and whittlers" arriving in two days. The elderly couples traveled as a group to Abagail's each fall and pursued their cherished activities: the husbands were deposited on the porch with pocket knives and sticks, while the wives swarmed Irish's kitchen to make jams and jellies for Christmas gifts. Using frozen fruits and canned juices that had been stocked away for their visit, the women preserved and sealed hundreds of fancy jars.

Irish hadn't told Max about the wives—ten women who didn't like men in the kitchen. During their stay, they would hand Irish grocery lists and shoo her from their realm. Wearing huge aprons with pockets, they'd serve the guests "down home" meals until their bus arrived to whisk them back to their condos.

"Do you realize how dangerous a fall would be to you or the baby?" Max demanded, carrying her along the wide porch. "Irish, Jeff has a highly paid maintenance crew." He paused, nudging aside a huge potato that had rolled from a gunnysack propped against the wall. The scent of fresh apples rose from the two bushel baskets near the potato sack, blending with the pungent odor of big sweet onions in another sack.

Irish gritted her teeth, brushing a long winding curl from her throat. Max's eyes darkened when she tucked it into the ponytail, and Irish suddenly remembered that the first button was missing from the shirt she had borrowed from him. "If anything happened to the baby, you'd really feel obligated to me, wouldn't you? Max, we're expecting a houseful of people in less than a week for Abagail's Fall Fiesta."

Max's mouth tightened grimly. "Shouldn't you be showing off new maternity clothes? What are you wearing to the Box Lunch social? This?" He hooked a finger in the worn flannel shirt and tugged.

Settling down in his arms, Irish tried to minimize the deep cleavage soaring up from her neckline. "It's never been a problem before."

Max lifted one eyebrow, bleached by the sun, and glanced at her chest. "You've changed, heart of mine. Though you always were delectable."

"Max..." Just then Max sat slowly, easing himself and Irish into her grandmother's refinished cherrywood rocker.

"Shh," he said against her temple, gathering her closer and beginning to rock.

Mimi wandered lazily across the porch in front of them, holding her tail high. She twitched the tip, and a parade of scrambling mewing kittens followed in her wake. Plopping down on a sun-warmed board, the barn cat meowed and rolled on her side, exposing the kitten's dinner. In a flash the kittens found her milk, their tiny paws pushing against her stomach.

Licking the kittens as they nursed, Mimi then stretched out to luxuriate in motherhood.

Unshed tears burned at the back of Irish's lids, and she allowed them to flow down her cheeks. The baby kicked pleasantly along her side, wanting more rocking, and Irish sniffed. "I hate being a weepy wimp," she whispered, admitting it aloud to Mimi—not to Max.

Max eased her head to his shoulder and continued rocking slowly. Being the tired limp-wimp that she was, Irish let herself slide into the security of Max's comfortably padded body.

Tucking his chin over her head, Max murmured, "If anyone calls you a wimp, leave them to me."

Irish swallowed and sniffed, fighting the smile toying along her lips. The image of Max dressed for a duel was impressive. As he had been when he'd kissed the head nurse's cheek after the Pickles and Peanut Butter tea. Ms. MacMannis had actually blushed. "Did you ask her to marry you?" the nurse had asked after tugging Max down by his collar to her level.

When he'd nodded, the starchy little nurse had patted him on the head. "Good boy. You'll do."

A serene delight had slid into his expression, and the nurse had nudged Irish. "We call that the 'new father glow.'"

Rocking in his arms, Irish wiped her cheek with the collar of his shirt, and Max lifted her palm to his lips. "Protection from wimpdom comes with a marriage certificate."

"Stop pushing, Max. Shotgun weddings aren't my favorite subject right now," Irish returned too quickly, instantly regretting it. But she wasn't comfortable with the situation. She just couldn't manage to tell her parents; once they knew, Max was in danger of extinction. He really hadn't done anything wrong—he, his potent genes and chromosomes had just come swooshing out of the Rockies at the wrong time. Now Max loomed at her side, pampering and understanding—a tower of strength.

He made her feel like a real wimp.

She'd never needed anyone really, just fluttering along through life passing out hugs and kisses. When she'd needed to be strong and fight for a cause, she had. But now Max was scooping everything away from her and replacing it with something else.

While Irish dealt with role reversal, a muscle moved in Max's hard cheek as he pressed his lips together. "A shotgun wedding—I don't like the sound of that. No one is forcing you to do anything."

Swept by the light breeze, a huge dry maple leaf rattled on the porch boards. Max rocked her slowly, locked in his thoughts, and the baby settled peacefully into his warm nest. Irish wanted to know more about Max. His warmth contradicted what little she knew of his past. She'd hurt him just then, she knew, aching for whatever Max kept wrapped so tightly inside.

She'd had a glimpse of it during the storm and hadn't liked what she'd found.

Max shifted her slightly, arranging her legs across his— the elevated-leg remedy. The rocker creaked steadily, the same noise at the exact place, and Irish relaxed against him. The peaceful moment stretched, running along into the autumn air as though it could last forever.

Then he said, "Marry me, Irish," and destroyed the first peace she'd felt since Max had stepped into the hospital's room of married parents-to-be.

Seven

The small room was soft with October light filtering in through the window. Max adjusted the shelf he'd made against the nursery wall. The baby's eye-coordination muscles would strengthen when he looked at the objects Max intended to place on the shelf. Smiling to himself, Max mocked the use of *he*. Irish didn't want to know the sex of the baby and neither did he.

Gauging the distance from the crib to the shelf again, Max stood back to view the effect of the maple wood against the tiny dancing bears.

Since the bus had arrived with the "spit and whittlers," Max had sought privacy in the greenhouse and Link's cluttered woodworking shop. The maple shelf was his first project from scratch, his gift to the baby. Max eased the shelf an eighth of an inch higher on the right side, leveling it. With the installation of humidity and temperature controls, the nursery would be perfect.

The aroma of apple dumplings and plum jam rose up the stairway, and he sniffed appreciatively. From the cassette player on the dresser, Brahms's violins floated over the nursery. Machine-gun sounds from Granny's printer in the computer room shot from the intercom, punctuating the classical movements. Max turned up the volume on the wall unit, listening to Granny mutter about the "damned bear market."

"What's the problem?" he asked, then bit into the zucchini bread a jam-making guest had slipped him out of guilt. After all, they had seized his new copper pots and owed him the tasty rental fee.

"Pork bellies are down a quarter. Stock in communications rising. Don't people know what's important?" Granny demanded hotly. "Pork bellies are where it's at."

Another refugee from the kitchen, Granny had attached herself to Max's computer room. Under Max's direction, she'd taken to stock indexes like the proverbial duck to water. With a grade-school education, the elderly woman had raised eight children and now looked at a promising future in stocks and bonds. Her portfolio was tidy and growing, and Link called her "The Whiz." Link had a promising future of his own. Max and Link had talked with a local radio station, and now Link's fishing reports were carried after the morning news.

Following Max's text for computer bookkeeping, The Whiz had started logging in payments and receipts. With that skill under her massive apron, she'd moved on to the guest register and payment system.

Granny could be a nightmare when she wanted to evict Irish's nonpaying guests. Recovering from a wayward husband and debts left in his wake, Liz Fredell had received a free pass from Irish. While the woman was on a mountain trail ride, Granny had packed her bags and cleaned the room. "Fredell is out of here," the farm woman had told Max, crossing her arms.

Realizing how Irish would react—citing him as a bad, negative, money-picking influence—Max bribed Granny with a new stock-communications computer system and had supplied payment for Liz. When the elderly jam-makers migrated back to their tour bus, Max could have his kitchen back and revert to swaying Granny with pâtés, stuffed grape leaves and anything with nuts floating in a flaming brandy sauce.

Granny continued muttering through the intercom, and Max interrupted, "Check the penny stock. You might be encouraged there," Max said.

"Hey, Max, I got a lead on some hot stocks. Stop in when you get time—tell me what you think. I scanned Jeff's figures on labor and repair to the combine—they don't jibe with the mechanic's bill. Looks like the numbers have been doctored with carbon paper."

Max's mouth tightened. A tracer on the manager had turned up a tidy rap sheet, including a sentence for check forgery.

He watched the bear mobile dance over the crib. A confrontation with Jeff now wouldn't help Irish. He'd pushed Jeff just enough to let him know that he was being watched.

The Whiz repeated his thoughts over the intercom. "Don't worry. I remember what you said about not upsetting Irish, but she knows a scam is up... Nadia left a message for you to call her at the cottage.... My broker's morning report is coming in. Catch you later, 'gator."

Switching the wall unit to the cottage intercom, Max waited for Nadia to answer. A storm of Gypsy curses—Nadia had gleaned them from a textbook—crackled over the intercom. *"What!"*

Max dusted the last of the zucchini-bread crumbs from his fingers. "You wanted me?"

Turning down the volume, he waited until she had paused for breath. Then she began again and Max felt obliged to say "uh-huh...uh-huh..." in the proper places. According to Nadia, the latest research on crystals and the psyche must have been written by a baboon dining on funny weed, not a true medium. She intended to call out the author for a crystal and tarot-card showdown.

"Uh-huh," Max agreed dutifully as a movement beyond the window caught his attention. "In your book, why don't you list the author as a source, then go on to contradict him with your personal experiences, Nadia?" he suggested absently, moving the curtain aside to watch Irish below.

As Irish walked to the barn, the slight autumn wind caught the dark gold fields sweeping out behind her and rippled through them. Aspen leaves trembled, shimmering and riding the breeze as it swept upward to the mountain pines.

The breeze lifted and tossed Irish's hair; the bright reddish gold mass caught the sun and played with it. A long curl blew across her cheek, and she carelessly brushed it aside. Pasted against her body by the wind, her denim coat outlined the gentle mound of her stomach.

Dressed in jeans and joggers, carrying a small basket of apples for the horses, the mother of his child fitted beautifully into the timeless rustic scene under the shadow of the majestic Rockies.

But he was running out of time.

The mother of his child, Max repeated mentally as maple leaves skipped across the lawn to riffle at her feet. She was more than that. She was the warmth of his life, a combination of sunlight and flowers.

The Van Damme loveless hearts wouldn't touch her or his child.

Max's hand tightened on the back of the rocking chair; he realized suddenly that he'd been gripping it tightly, the wood cutting into his palm.

Fate had given them a child. Max swallowed the dry wad of fear in his throat. Dangling just beyond his experience, a tiny word—love—taunted him.

He hadn't known love. How would he recognize it? How would he give it?

Irish and the baby deserved to be wrapped in love, given by a man who knew how to love. *Could he?*

Fear, unbidden and wild, went slithering through him. Tucked into Irish's TLC domain, Max was a trespasser without credentials. He slowly uncurled his fingers from the chair. Degrees in loving weren't handed out easily, and he might not qualify.

Max had never waited for anything; he'd plunged through his career, methodically lining up the facts and getting results. Experienced and skilled at his work, Max had never relied on his loving instincts, and now Irish needed them.

He'd never been vulnerable and helpless in his lifetime. And he'd never felt more inadequate to a challenge.

In the autumn sunlight, Irish ran her hand over her stomach and smiled softly, talking to the baby—his child.

Max's mouth tightened. *How badly he wanted that tiny part of himself.* The fierce need to hold Irish, sharing the baby, ran through him like warm pungent wine.

Closing his eyes, Max ignored the burning behind his lids, the dampness oozing out to his lashes. Emotion sliced through him, and his hands trembled. He leaned back against the wall and listened to the uneven beat of his heart. He'd never listened to it before, never felt the hard lonely thud in his chest.

He didn't want to be alone again.

Max ran his hand across the antique dresser he'd just refinished. Carried upstairs from the basement, the cherrywood had responded to tung oil and hand rubbing, and now it gleamed richly in the muted light. He smiled slightly, warmed by the gift from the past.

Since he'd met Irish, he'd developed a feeling of belonging in this special place. With Irish.

Outside, the whittlers had started a musical-spoon symphony. Oddly enough, the beat seemed to blend with the sounds of Brahms.

Sitting on the rocker, Max listened to its comforting squeak-squeak noise. Then he leaned his head against the back of the chair and watched the bears dance and thought about Irish.

In her sixth month of pregnancy, she was more delicious than when he'd first met her. Irish's fresh-faced, all-American look had been replaced by a sultry exotic beauty that could stun a man at fifty paces. Beneath a mass of curls, her eyes had darkened to a luminous blue, and her lips had taken on a dewy softness. Max didn't want her stunning men without him at her side. The thoughts of another man parenting his baby caused Max to break out in a cold sweat. But if Nadia's predictions were on course, Irish should be weakening soon.

He rubbed his stomach uneasily. Lately it had had a tight uncomfortable feeling as if he'd eaten too much. Maybe it was all that sexual energy wadded into one tight ball.

He'd kept his distance, giving Irish the breathing space she needed. But space between them had cost him. Max smiled grimly at the huge panda lounging in a corner. In trading his Porsche for a station wagon, he'd picked up values he'd once considered old-fashioned. Sleeping alone in the cottage wasn't easy, but Irish had been compromised enough.

Lounging amidst the cottage's bedroom mirrors, the madam's portrait reminded him of Irish—sexy, warm and knowing how to love. Lying across her pillows, swathed in a transparent scarf, the madam mocked his celibacy. Once he'd found himself standing in front of the climbing rose trellis leading up to Irish's room.

Max reached for a flannel receiving blanket and wrapped a fuzzy blue bear in it. Holding the bear against his stomach eased the tight empty feeling.

Max traced the bears dancing from the crib's tiny mobile. He'd been like that, never touching the ground or staying in one place for long. He'd never wanted the white picket fence, the American apple-pie dream. Nothing but his career had mattered. But now lying within his grasp was a life with Irish, and Max wanted it desperately.

As owner of the inn, Irish could toss him out at any time, and the thought terrified him. Max had grown to like the shotgun-wedding idea; writing Irish's parents that he intended to marry their daughter was a stroke of genius.

Ida and Ruben Dalton, Florida retirees, had once owned a small vineyard. Katherine had tossed him the idea in an offhand remark about how her parents would love immediately any man who knew how to make wine.

According to his research, a small winery near the inn was possible with irrigation. Granny had located an acreage bordering Abagail's and had gotten Max a good price for the land.

Rocking slowly, Max thought of holding his baby in the middle of the night. Patting the bear's bottom, he thought of holding Irish anytime he could.

She fitted into his life with a softness that filled his heart.

In the room next to the nursery, Irish stripped in front of the full-length mirror. According to Max's chart, she'd gained twelve pounds. All of them pressed tightly against her white cotton briefs and bra.

She ran her palm over the small mound and was rewarded by a small kick. Turning to the side, Irish studied her body. She'd always been...rounded, she decided benignly and hoped that the cocoa butter helped freckles stretch, too.

"Pudgy," she muttered, turning her back to the mirror. Her breasts ballooned over the edge of her bra, which had been loosened to the last loops.

She'd never been interested in fashion or investing time and energy in getting the "right look." But Max hadn't seemed to mind; of course he was obligated to compliment her—a happy mother's disposition was good for the baby. Those fond pats to her bottom when no one was looking were designed to make her feel feminine—another part of Max's expectant-mother program, added to the blood-pressure and diet charts. As the responsible paternal party, Max cheerfully monitored her body systems, poking a thermometer into her mouth if she sneezed and measuring her waist every two weeks.

She didn't want those brotherly kisses he'd been serving.

She turned her back to the mirror in a Betty Grable pose and tried her sexiest look. She wet her lips, parted them and leaned her head back, fluttering her eyelashes. A plain old earth mother stared back at her, rounded from shoulders to thighs. If ever she'd wanted to wear fancy black lace panties and bra to excite a man, it was now—when she felt like a potato and Max wasn't giving her those seductive kisses. In fact, Max was keeping his distance. She sniffed, ignoring the lively music of fiddles, and spoons clicking to the beat, beneath her window.

Max said he wanted to marry her. Good old Max, trying to make her *feel* as though she was beautiful, spreading his compliments around like Granny's favorite pâté. Good old Max, squiring her on medicinal twenty-minute walks every morning and evening. In another month, he wouldn't be able to stretch his arm around her waist. Max's hand always seemed to slide lower, riding her hips and smoothing them. Irish frowned at that rounded curve, suspiciously spotting what she thought was another fleshy inch.

She did like those walks, being tucked close to the safety of his chest and the scents of his after-shave caused little excited tremors to race through her—or was it her disturbed hormones? She wanted to wake up to those scents and tremors every morning and pat his freshly showered back dry. Irish closed her eyes, remembering Max's back—

wide shoulders with muscles that rippled beneath dark skin, tapering down to the cutest little dimple....

Sleeping wasn't easy in an ex-bordello, she'd discovered. The nuances of past lovers clung to walls, steeping her in restless wistful dreams. Before Max had zoomed into the valley in his Porsche she'd slept marvelously well. She'd practically dozed through the early part of her pregnancy, but now the nights were endless—even with the baby's comforting kicks. She'd begun to think of ways to seduce Max back into her bed—just to have him near her. "Oh, spare me, Irish. How low can you get?" she asked the reflection. "You've never played the femme fatale, and now your equipment isn't exactly in champion shape."

She turned to the side, viewing her eggplant shape intently. "I miss sleeping on my stomach," she muttered, remembering cuddling to Max's sturdy back. She'd tried the giant panda in the nursery, but somehow fuzzy cloth wasn't like rippling muscle and warm skin.

Max's reverent kisses may have slipped over the edge to sensual once or twice, but for the most part, he was keeping his distance.

No one was letting her do all the things she loved—cooking special dishes, serving apple cider to the guests, cleaning and freshening the rooms. All those little cherishy things she loved to do for her guests were outlawed, tabooed and generally dismissed. "Put your feet up, rest awhile," she repeated darkly. Link's comments were always prime—"Take some weight off your feet."

"Hell's bells, stop whining, lady." Irish scowled at the mirror. She wasn't into scooping up sacrificial males, no matter how well they carried off the attentive father-to-be role.

Obligation now wouldn't keep Max happy later, she reminded herself again. Nobility could be stretched only so far, then it would snap, and Max would find himself in a situation he wouldn't want for a lifetime.

A long curl slid across her cheek, and Irish blew it out of the way. She'd meant to cut her hair, but somehow never found the time. Irish thrust it into a ponytail high on her head, tied a blue ribbon into the wild curly mass and studied the effect. She didn't look like a woman who would suit Max—sleek worldly Max. She looked like a freckle-faced young girl with huge eyes and a soft vulnerable mouth. Or like a woman who didn't have a clue in the world how to appeal to a man like Max. Of course he tried to make her *feel* as if she were a crepe instead of a pancake. But then there was that obligation thing of his. "The old ball and chain," she muttered.

While she struggled to keep from waddling, Max had begun to swagger just a tad, she decided moodily. Shielded in his new rugged Western look, he'd developed into a warm friendly person with a sense of humor. Those laughter lines were deepening beside his eyes; his mouth had lost that flat hard edge. And the cutest little twinkle flirted with her from his dark brown eyes.

She rubbed her stomach, easing the tightened skin. When Max did laugh, the rich genuine sound warmed her clear through. Last night Link played his harmonica, and Max had instigated a kitchen hoedown with the ladies from the bus, and Granny and Nadia. The impromptu dance squashed a hot skirmish over paraffin options for jars of apple butter. When he'd spotted Irish, his eyes had darkened and he'd swung her gently against him. His kiss had been long and searching, so intensely hungry that she'd barely heard the ladies' wistful oohs and ahhs.

Max had traded in his calculator-for-a-heart image for... the happy-daddy look that tracked her every movement.

How was she going to manage watching Max hold the baby, caring for him when he grew? What if Max found someone else?

Someone lean and stylish who wasn't shaped like an eggplant.

Irish sniffed again and turned toward the bed. Strewn across it was an assortment of new maternity clothes, from casual to dressy. Across one T-shirt, big wide letters screamed, "Baby Cargo."

Caressing the baby, Irish whispered, "Don't get the wrong idea down there. You're wanted very much. It's just that your daddy isn't obliged to marry me. I can putt along without his sympathy."

Allowing herself one more sniff, Irish began trying on clothes. Katherine had sent boxes from Denver's exclusive shops, a sisterly gift. While Irish preferred T-shirts, sweatshirts and jeans, Katherine's taste ran to sweaters and jumpers, trim business suits and designer jeans. These clothes however, ran to frilly lace, ruffles and tiny splashes of nosegays on blue and pink backgrounds.

Irish lifted the pink maternity jumper to study it, then she frowned. Katherine, a sleek blonde, wasn't the type to choose the old-fashioned country-girl look. Nor was she likely to buy jumpers with bears scooting around on tricycles, or fluorescent maternity sweatsuits with "Call Me Mommy" in big letters across the chest.

Irish held up a lacy white dress. Cut in a simple princess style with a wide collar and long puffy sleeves, the dress was exquisite right down to its big satin bow at the bodice. Katherine had pinned a tag on it—"From me to you." Another tag slithered from the folds of the next box from a lingerie shop—Katherine's elegant script read, "Go get him, sis."

Carefully folded between sheaths of tissue paper, a pale blue teddy with an expandable front panel rested in all its transparent glory. "She's certainly picked the wrong time to develop her sense of humor. Max hasn't even come close to me."

Irish lifted an immense bra to her chest and groaned. "Great. Just what I need—room for expansion."

Taking a deep steadying sigh, Irish grabbed a dress, took a courageous breath and dived into it.

Tiny white sprigs danced around the loose blue cotton, and white lace skittered around the wide collar and sleeves. The tiny pearl buttons on the puffy sleeves matched the buttons at the throat. The bodice clung to her chest and draped loosely down her legs. The bow stuck out from her chest like a pom-pom.

Irish sniffed back a sob, smoothing the strings of the pom-pom. Max, in his obligated kindness, hadn't mentioned her breasts or parts south. But there they were, like two huge balloons.

In fact, Max hadn't touched her anywhere but at her back. He probably couldn't find her waist. Oh, he may have sighed a little when he gave her an obligatory hug. And no doubt his uneven breath was from the effort. And the trembling, too.

Irish blinked back a tear. She couldn't blame him for not wanting her. She'd grabbed his fifty-to-one chance of pregnancy and run with it like an experienced quarterback with a football.

She didn't want to answer the knock at her bedroom door.

"Honey," a woman's voice called softly.

"Mother!" she exclaimed just as the door swung open to reveal her parents.

"My little girl!" Her father's outraged tone swept into the room.

"Baby," her mother cried softly, her eyes widening on Irish's maternity dress. "My sweet little innocent baby girl . . ."

Max entered the scenario, standing a head above her parents. In the shadows of the hallway, his expression was grim and his body rigid. "Irish is having my baby."

Much shorter, her father pivoted slowly as though at any moment he'd reach for the nonexistent six-shooter at his hip. "*You* sent the letter. You're Van Damme. I'm Ruben Dalton, Irish's father," he said in a deadly tone, spelling out his parental rights to the usurper. "Irish Serene is my daughter."

"She's my baby girl," Ida added in a righteous tone to the seducer of her child.

Max smiled his warmest, most devastating new-father best down at her parents. "I want to marry her. She isn't buying."

A collection of the tour couples had gathered in the hallway. "Marry the poor guy," an elderly gentleman leaning on a cane called.

"The baby needs a name," a dignified gray-haired giantess added.

"The baby has my name," Max said, smiling benignly in his supreme confidence. "It's a formality that the baby takes the father's name."

"Try again, son," a retired attorney stated quietly. He nodded toward Irish. "Mama there holds the reins."

"My grandson deserves the best," Ruben began huffily, turning to his wife. "Ida, make plans to move from Florida. My grandson needs someone to raise him and I guess it will have to be me," he ordered, glaring up at Max. "A boy can't just be tossed into the world. He needs to know how to catch trout and slide into first base..."

"I know how to fish and play ball," Max said between his teeth, returning the glare.

Ruben looked up Max's tall body, then back down. "Bet you can't slide into base worth a hoot. You're a damned foreigner to this grand state of Colorado. A city slicker to boot. Throw in making your living with a computer and what do you get?" he asked, his face coloring with anger. "Some fly-by-night yahoo—"

"Pop," Ida interrupted softly just as the tears came to Irish's eyes. "Look how pretty she is in a dress and her hair in a ribbon. Our little girl—"

"She's the most beautiful woman in the world," Max stated emphatically. Then he loomed down over the smaller man and ground his teeth a moment before saying very quietly, "Could we continue this later? The guests are here for peace and quiet."

"No, we're not," three of the grandmotherly types returned. "Go right on ahead. I know a lot about this situation—went through it with my daughter, and her marriage turned out just fine."

Ida moved into the room and smiled at Irish. "Hello, honey," she said, brushing a curl back from her daughter's hot cheek.

The two men, keeping a wary distance between each other, stepped into the room and closed the door.

Max stopped, shot a hard assessing glance at Irish, then moved swiftly to pick her up. Too tired to deal with a full-fledged Dalton-style hullabaloo, Irish simply leaned her head against Max's safe shoulder as he lifted her into his arms. He tensed, holding her tightly against him. Then he kissed her cheek once and her lips twice in short bits of care that soothed her rumpled nerves. Max moved to an old rocker and sat in it, still holding Irish. Ignoring her parents, he kissed her a third time, more slowly, tenderly.

Irish found herself responding, lifting her lips to receive his kiss. She cradled Max's jaw with her palm, soothing him. "I'll protect you," she offered, kissing his hard cheek.

In the background her father moved restlessly. *"Protect him?"*

Her mother pushed aside the maternity clothing on the bed and sat watching them closely. "I'm really good at putting on weddings, Max," she offered quietly. "With all my experience, I could throw one together in half a day—a day at the most—with everyone's help."

Irish let herself fall into Max's warm gaze; Max looked at her as though he'd just discovered ice cream—the interesting double-dutch-cherry-nut kind. She saw herself in his eyes as they moved over her face and hair, taking in the jumbled curls and the feminine lacy collar. His gaze swept slowly down her loose dress, his mouth beginning to curve in a wolfish smile.

In another instant, they were alone with Ruben's muffled outrage and Ida's soothing tones coming from the hallway. When the lock clicked, Irish whispered shakily, "She's locked us in. She used to do that to Katherine and me when we fought. We made up just to see daylight again."

She blushed as Max's fingers found the bow and prowled around it. "I've never seen you in anything but pants—or nothing but freckles," he added naughtily. "Don't be shy, Irish," he said in a low hungry drawl that deepened her blush.

"I'm bosomy," she said.

"Mmm, sexy." Max stood and carried her to the bed.

"Max..." she protested weakly as he placed her on the bed and stretched out beside her. "Max..." she whispered shakily as his eyes darkened to silky black, his expression intent as he leaned over her. His fingers played with the bow and the lace, tormenting her sensitive breasts.

"Marry me, Irish," he murmured, lowering his head to kiss her lips.

While Irish hazily tried to find reality, Max's lips were building his case. They slid across her hot cheeks and down her throat where he had just unbuttoned and exposed new grazing area. She swallowed, trying to keep her traitorous senses on a level keel, but they kept shifting and heating.

"You're beautiful," he murmured in the proximity of her collarbone, his hand slowly lifting the hem of the dress to find her thigh. His mouth found hers again, brushing tempting little unsatisfying kisses across it.

Her fingers had somehow found all that nice hair covering his chest and were rummaging through it. Somehow her other hand was trailing through his crisp hair, mussing it and finding the way it curled to the back of his strong neck. Between kisses, she looked up at Max's flushed intent face and whispered, "You don't have to do this, Max. My parents will migrate back to Florida when they see they can't have their way."

Breathing heavily, Max ran his hand up her thigh and across the baby nestling in her. When he rubbed the small mound, the kicking movements stilled. "I put him back to sleep," he whispered proudly. "I've got the daddy touch. I could put him to sleep every night if you'll marry me," he whispered, foraging with tiny kisses a direct trail toward the spot behind her ear.

But Irish wanted his lips on hers, wanted the taste of his hunger. Max allowed her to draw him back, to nibble on his lips while his fingers eased open her tiny pearl buttons. When he held back the kiss she wanted desperately, Max ran his finger around her sensitized lips, tugging at the bottom one. "Marry me," he urged, the dark passion in his eyes igniting her hunger.

"No, Max. Marriage for the baby's sake or mine isn't necessary," she managed huskily.

"It's necessary for me," he stated roughly, just before his mouth took hers fully.

The kiss was long and devastating. Her theory that she could manage without Max shot out into the sweeping autumn wind. When she tugged him closer, Max resisted.

When she moved to pull him back, he whispered, "Marry me."

"Yes, Max."

After a deep kiss that stoked their hunger, Max forced himself away from her. Irish snuggled to his side, the eggplant and balloon syndromes kissed away. When she pressed a kiss to his damp chest—his shirt had been opened somehow—Max groaned shakily, stilling her wandering fingers. "How fast did your mother say she could put a wedding together?"

Eight

"What am I doing?" A week later, Irish gripped the stairway handrail tightly with her left hand, the one with Max's heirloom-style engagement ring on it. The afternoon light coming from the stained-glass window caught the heart-shaped diamond and sent out myriad colors. Through her wedding veil, the expressions of her family and friends looking up at her ranged from wistful to delighted. The inn's antique organ played the "Wedding March," and the white dress Katherine had given her slid silkily over a lace maternity teddy.

Irish listened to her heart beat heavily. She gripped the frothy bouquet of pink roses and white daisies tightly and swallowed. The movement lifted the antique sapphire necklace Max had sent to her just before the wedding. She blinked, fighting back tears. Sapphires and roses weren't her style, more fitting for a model on the cover of a bridal magazine. Yet the stones matched the current shade of her eyes, bringing out the dewy dark blue color, and the pink roses were exactly the color of her cheeks—beneath the freckles. Piled high on her head, her long curls danced when she turned, tiny tendrils fluttering at the back of her neck. Taking a last look in the full-length mirror earlier, she'd realized she looked radiant beneath the bridal veil.

In the past week she'd been pampered and shushed and shooed away from anything that resembled work. Katherine, her mother, Granny and Nadia had jumped into action, inviting neighbors, relatives and a collection of her favorite guests. The ten couples had stayed past their checkout date; the women bustled through the house making tiny candies and comparing cake, punch and groom's-cake recipes. The men, including J.D., had equaled the tasks under Ida's and Granny's direction. Katherine had been placed in charge of Irish's uncertain temperament and had advised Max to keep his distance.

Throughout the hectic week, Max remained serene, his checklists thrusting from his pockets, and his eyes tracking Irish. Her father grumbled that the cart had been placed before the horse. But he liked Max—who had apparently passed the "What're your intentions for my little girl?" test.

The full-scale wedding was the combined effort of the two males. Her father was adamant about escorting his baby girl down the aisle, and Max couldn't be swayed into a practical civil ceremony. He wanted a traditional wedding: ribbons, baskets of roses and daisies, beeswax candles and French champagne served in long-stemmed crystal glasses. He'd insisted that a seamstress add another lacy tier to the dress.

Tonight she'd share the cottage with Max; her parents would use her room for the duration of their visit. No doubt Max had been properly threatened by her father and Katherine. Everything was arranged.

There was no going back. *Did she want to?*

Somehow she'd jumped through time zones, shucked her jeans and T-shirt and slithered into bridal white lace and a coronet of pink baby roses and daisies. Her wedding would serve as the kickoff to Abagail's Fall Fiesta.

Irish couldn't worry about Abagail's now; she had to think of herself. And Max. And the baby.

Poor Max. Pressured by his own code of ethics, he was obliged to marry her, a temporary patch on a bad situation. He couldn't possibly love her now, just at the waddly-pudgy stage. Max was gallant; he wanted to shield her from gossip and protect the baby, too.

But that wasn't love.

Max was performing exactly like he thought he should, right down to the wedding.

When would he discover his mistake? He'd wake up one morning and wonder why he'd been so noble.

At least he hadn't lied by telling her of a love that didn't exist. Max was too noble to lie, too upright to leave her in a maternity bridal gown.

Frantic, Irish shivered, looking down at her father who waited at the bottom of the stairs. Without Max, she could have managed her life and the baby's....

The minister waited in the parlor. The matron of honor, Katherine, and the best man, J.D., stood beside him.

Max needed someone to really love. Not a marriage trap. He couldn't say he loved her—because he didn't. One day he'd hate her....

Irish swallowed again.

As if reminded of his father, the baby kicked impatiently against her side. Then Irish started slowly down the stairs to take Ruben's arm.

Max waited with the minister, Katherine and J.D. Her mother sniffed from the rows of folding chairs, and her father's hand gripped hers tightly. Dressed in a gray tuxedo, Maxwell Van Damme was elegant, and the sight of him made her heart beat faster and the baby kick frantically. His eyes flickered over her, and his harsh features seemed to soften. She met his eyes, holding them as she walked slowly to his side, leaving her father's hand.

The wedding vows were spoken, her voice husky as she answered the minister's questions. Then Max was lifting her veil, taking her gently into his arms and kissing her sweetly as though she were his heart, his love.

Oh, he had to do that for appearances, she thought distantly. When his arm kept her close, Irish ached with the bittersweet pain. Ached for Max and the charade she'd put him through. She almost sobbed when he kissed away a tear.

Nadia caught the bouquet. Rafe, J.D.'s handsome brother, caught the blue garter from her leg, and Jonathan had arrived to take formal wedding pictures. Mac, J.D.'s other brother, and his wife, Diana, helped Granny and Link serve the guests at the reception.

Later, alone in the cottage—he'd insisted on carrying her over the threshold—Max's kisses changed and became filled with an immediate hunger she returned. "At last," he murmured softly, lifting the rose buds from her hair. Max carefully removed the pins holding her ringlets on top of her head and dropped them to the floor.

Finding the teddy beneath her gown, Max's darkened gaze caressed the lace slowly, intently. "Cute," he said softly, slipping a finger under the strings and tugging them free. "But freckles are better."

During the long exquisite night, Max kept her close and kissed away her tears.

Two days later, Irish tidied up the cottage, left a note for Max and set out for her favorite thinking spot in a stand of aspens. Max, Ida and Ruben were off to his "vineyards," leaving her to sleep. She'd badly needed the time alone. Somehow no one needed her anymore. The guests were fiesta-ing themselves silly with barbecues, whittling contests, hoedowns, and had generally run over the inn.

Irish walked through high dry weeds, gathering her coat around her. Clouds skimmed the sky, sweeping shadows across the craggy mountains. A deer leapt gracefully over a bubbling stream on its way to a field. A hawk soared high in the sky, screeching, and aspen leaves crackled beneath her feet.

The arrival of her parents had tripped off a fast pace, and Max hadn't given her a quiet moment to think.

Max was acting exactly like a new bridegroom should—if only she didn't feel that he was only trying to reassure her parents.

On the ski slope, workmen were testing the lifts.

The new cables were to have been installed and running properly for guests who wanted to take in the panoramic views. Irish paused, brushing a curl back from her face as she watched the laborious climb of the empty seats up the slope. The movement was jerky, the machinery fighting the cables.

Picking her way across a rock embankment, Irish headed toward the small shed housing the motor. Jeff met her at the doorway, wiping his oily hands on a rag. "Hi, Irish."

His eyes ran down her body like slimy hands, and Irish suddenly remembered his furious expression at the wedding. Then she'd been too wrapped up in her own emotions, but now seemed a perfect time to talk with him. "Hello, Jeff. How's it going?"

"Going fine. The men have just put in the new cable...." He paused when Irish's gaze skimmed the rusty worn cable. Before Max's precise notations, she'd left the machinery and fields to Jeff while she'd maintained the inn and near grounds.

"A new cable?" she repeated, running her fingers along a length and looking down at the rust on them.

Jeff's hard face flushed, and his eyes brightened with anger. "Look, you just keep Van Damme happy and keep him out of my business," he snarled, shifting into a defensive stance. "You get pregnant—the guy naturally feels obligated to stick around until the kid is born. Hell, he even does his duty and marries you, but that isn't any reason for me to put up with him. He's been sticking his nose into my business. That's why I got those blueprints from his house."

"You went into the cottage?"

"Damn right. Got worked over for it, too. Van Damme wouldn't have touched me, but he's got these foreign moves. The guy's not human, except when it comes to you. A regular machine. Keep him away from me."

"Max had a right to protect his privacy, Jeff. You had no right to pilfer."

A cold wind swept up her neck and she shivered. Jeff's angry accusation mirrored her thoughts while she'd walked. With her parents arriving on Abagail's doorstep, Max was compromised into marrying her. Of course, he hadn't wanted her to be uncomfortable, and the wedding solved everyone's problems but hers. She didn't want him trussed and stuffed and serve up into a marriage without... without what Max deserved most—lots of love.

She crushed a thistle stalk in her hand, ignoring the tiny thorns prickling her skin. Max had been forced by his personal code to stand before a minister and promise to love her.

What did he really feel?

Max hadn't said he loved her; she hadn't expected it.

Irish shivered, realizing how deeply Max had infiltrated her heart.

The cable creaked loudly, bringing Irish's thoughts back to Jeff. Suddenly all the discrepancies in Jeff's stories about his needy family fell into neat little shards at his feet.

She hadn't seen Jeff's livid anger before and now that she had, Irish didn't like it.

She touched the cable, and when she held up her hand, the rust color was evident. Jeff scowled and tossed the rag aside. "Yeah, so what?" he asked belligerently. "I've been running this place pretty damn good for years, and you're not ruining anything I've got going."

The game warden had come asking questions about Jeff's trips into the mountains with a group of male guests.

Trophy deer had been drugged and staked out for hunter's bullets, and hearsay had brought the law to Abagail's. Irish thought of the tractor, dying just past its warranty. Rather like a marriage after a beautiful wedding... "You're fired," she said quietly, looking up at him. "Leave your forwarding address with Granny—she'll see you get paid what's due you."

"The hell I am," he muttered, reaching for her. Then a shadow moved across Jeff's face, and Max stepped into view.

"That's enough," Max said quietly, placing his arm around Irish's shoulder and easing her aside.

Irish shook loose. "Stay out of this, Max," she said between her teeth, glaring at Jeff.

"Fine. When you cool down, you can handle it any way you want. But not now," he added, glancing at Jeff. Max took her hand in his and looked at Jeff. The air stilled between them; Max loomed dangerously over the smaller man. A taut muscle moved in his cheek. The veneer of civilization slipped from him, and he stood like a gunfighter, long legs locked and his hands hanging loosely by his sides. "You heard her. Go on."

In that instant, Irish thought of the mountain men and pioneers who had stood their ground, defending what was precious to them against enemies and the elements. The same fierce savagery, barely trimmed, skimmed along Max's hard face.

She swallowed, remembering all the gentle times. The same harsh dark eyes flickering dangerously at Jeff who had warmed her with tenderness.

Then she knew that Max had not revealed himself like that to anyone else; he'd kept that loving part of himself for her. Whatever it was that Max hoarded for her alone, she'd treasure.

After Jeff had skulked off, thinking better of tangling with Max, Irish shivered, suddenly realizing the dangerous position in which she'd placed the baby and herself. For a moment Jeff had terrified her and now, knees shaking, she felt the full impact.

"You came after me," she whispered, wrapping her arms around his waist.

"I'll always come after you." Taking her into his arms, Max held her quietly. Against her temple, he spoke in an uneven low raspy tone. "Dear heart, promise me you won't face anything or anyone in a situation like this without me. I couldn't bear losing... Just don't."

After a long while, he tipped her chin up. "Hey, we're partners, remember? Like Bogie and Bacall, Roy and Dale, the Marx brothers—"

She couldn't help grinning, wrapping her arms tightly around him. "There's three of them."

"And three of us," he murmured before kissing her.

"Psst. Max, are you busy?" The Whiz whispered from the intercom.

Max opened one eye, pulled Irish's warm soft body closer and nuzzled the jumble of curls lying across the pillow. He noted mentally that the next time he had Irish in his arms, there wouldn't be an intercom or a telephone in the room.

Irish mumbled about obligations and anchovies on whipped cream, rummaging for a pillow to put over her head.

"Psst," The Whiz insisted. "Got a glitch in the communications systems. Can't find out whether pork bellies are up or down. Think you can spare a minute to come over here?"

Shifting his thigh aside to allow for Irish's comfort, Max closed his eyes. "Do I have a choice?"

"Pork bellies are important, Max," The Whiz reasoned. "Tell you what. I'll cut you a deal you can't refuse. After the baby is born and Irish is back to feeling pert, Link and I will run the inn for a solid month while you hightail it out of here with your family. When the baby is old enough, we'll baby-sit while you ..."

At the inn, Max quickly answered The Whiz's questions, then started working on a breakfast tray for Irish. He'd wanted to serve her breakfast that first morning. Now three days later, he hadn't managed to leave her until it was time to have lunch with the guests and her family at the inn.

Her family. Irish had been raised in the warmth of a loving family. Ruben and Ida's love filled a room when they entered it. Katherine and Irish bantered, giggled and hugged.

Stirring the wooden spoon in the copper pot as the mixture thickened and ignoring the ringing telephone, Max wondered if Irish knew what she had cried out in the night. *Oh, Max, I love you ... love you ... love you.*

The soft passionate cry had gripped him in fear. He didn't want to hurt her. But he might. Irish needed everything a man with a loving heart could give.

Staring at the hot mixture, Max sorted methodically through his emotions. When he'd been alone, the absence of love in him hadn't mattered. But she needed to know that he cared. That she was the one shining thing to happen in his life.

Granny's voice slid into the kitchen from the intercom just as Max was flipping a crepe. "Personal call from Geneva on the line, Max. Sounds important."

He picked up the kitchen telephone while thickening the raspberry sauce. "Van Damme here."

"Max. This is Elena. How are you?" The voice of his mother caught Max in the stomach, reminding him that his world before Irish had been a cold and painful one. He placed the raspberry mixture aside and turned off the burner.

"I'm fine. How are you and Father?" A muscle tightened in his cheek and ran into his throat; Max rubbed his palm across the burning pain in his stomach. He didn't dislike his parents, but if Irish glimpsed the prominent Van Damme family trait...

"Excellent. Our genetic report on familial associations was well received. What projects are you working on? According to your message center in New York, you've been tied up on some rural Colorado project." Max frowned, noting that this was his mother's expression of caring—a periodical progress report that she could file under "Van Damme, Maxwell—Male Child."

At his side, a soft fragrance and a softer touch told him that Irish had entered the room. He couldn't hide his uneasiness that his parents might ruin the one relationship he wanted most in the world.

The Van Dammes weren't vicious people, but their lack of warmth could cut a loving heart to shreds; no one knew that better than he did. Placing his cheek in the curling reddish blond hair, he gathered Irish's softness against his side, shielding her. Or was he shielding himself?

Irish's comforting arms wrapped around him while he completed the necessary report. He omitted Irish and the baby as her hand gently rubbed his stomach. Then, when he replaced the telephone in its cradle, he realized he'd been trembling. "You're not going to tell them," Irish said quietly, her dark blue eyes looking up at him.

"No. Not now."

"Max," she whispered, leaning against him, "everything is going to be just fine."

"I don't want them near you. Or the baby," he said finally, realizing how poorly equipped he was to fight fear.

"Sweetheart," she murmured, resting her head on his shoulder. "Haven't I protected you against the Daltons?"

He wanted to smile, but the past lurked too near the treasure he'd just found. Irish leaned back and the bright jumble of her curls spilled over his arm, warming his flesh. She ran her hand down his cheek, caressing and soothing him. "Time to let go, Max," she whispered finally.

"No, I can't afford them touching my life now," he managed huskily. "Not even for you."

Once her parents had left for Florida, Irish was at Max's mercy again. Her father had gotten her a brief respite, claiming Max's attentions for the new vineyard partnership. They bickered pleasantly about top billing on the sign—Van Damme versus Dalton.

Her mother had offered brief protection when she'd snagged Max for an afternoon of creek fishing. Ida thought of Max as "just a little boy, cute as a button when he catches a fish. Can't wait for my grandson if he's anything like Max."

But now he was back in charge, discussing her examinations with Dr. Williams and making certain that she'd remembered her specimen jars.

At the evening organizational meeting of prepared-childbirth class, Max snarled at Nurse MacMannis, "No, I'm not going to drown the baby. Pick on someone your own size." The rubber doll he'd been bathing and diapering for twenty-two minutes squeaked, protesting his tight hold. J.D.'s gift to Max, the deluxe model of Baby-Wetcakes, promptly dampened Max's jeans in an inappropriate place.

"Get used to it. Comes with the territory," MacMannis crowed, shooting Irish a conspiratorial grin as Max frowned and dabbed at the wet spot. She nudged Max with her elbow. "It's November—she's in her seventh month, Max. Two more months and you'll be putting all this good training to use. You'll want to kiss me when it's over."

Max muttered a dark phrase about her kissing something, and the nurse grinned up at him. "Boy, do I love to get big macho guys like you in my childbirth classes. I can usually crack the cool prepared ones on the first night. Takes the starch out of 'em so they make better coaches."

Max shot Irish a look of pure fury.

She blew him back a kiss.

MacMannis kept the pressure on Max during the orientation session, and Irish kept on blowing him kisses. Caught between the curt demands of the starchy little nurse and the promise of Irish's kisses later, Max was delightfully confused.

When he botched a session of "slow deep chest breathing" with an improper count, MacMannis resorted to tapping him on the head. "Bad boy."

Later that night, Max threw the crumpled practice schedule onto the four-poster bed. "MacMannis is an animal. In the morning, I'm checking out her credentials as a qualified leader. Even her toenails better be squeaky clean. I think we should consider an apartment in Denver just before the baby is due. This whole thing needs a good working system."

Irish sat on the bed, propped up with pillows, and enjoyed the delightful sight of Max, rumpled and outraged, stalking across their bedroom floor. His fingers rummaged through the hair on his bare chest as he thought about ways to systemize MacMannis. The white boxer shorts set off his dark skin, fluttering against his hard thighs when he moved.

Running his hand across the stubble covering his jaw, Max paused. His gaze skimmed Irish's face, hesitated as though caught in the act of boiling the nurse in oil, then ran leisurely down the T-shirt covering her body to her legs. He returned her grin slowly. "You like her, don't you?"

"Uh-huh. It's been a hard day, hasn't it, Maxi?" In the hospital, he had paled and leaned against the wall when they'd passed the birthing room and a woman's high-pitched scream shot out into the hallway. First-time fathers-to-be were given a tiny newborn to hold, and Max had actually shuddered. He'd held the infant clumsily, letting the baby nuzzle on his shoulder. Just when Max had begun to relax, the baby had burped.

Walking slowly to the bed, Max looked down at her, his face in the shadows. "Irish, I'm not about to let anything happen to you. I'm serious about the Denver apartment. Or we could stay at your sister's. A hospital is just two miles from them."

She took his hand and drew him down beside her. Max had grown so necessary in her life, she thought, placing her cheek over his heart and listening to the comforting steady beat. She smoothed the hair on his chest, patting him. His fingers tangled in her hair, finding her scalp and rubbing it gently.

Foraging in the night, coyotes howled. Irish closed her eyes and drifted with the luxurious caress; no wonder Mimi ran to Max. "Everything will be fine, Max. You'll see. But if it makes you feel better you can have your helicopter pad."

He kissed her forehead. "Thanks. Can you promise me better treatment from MacMannis?"

The baby kicked against him, and Max placed his palm over it. His awed expression tugged at Irish and she stroked his hair.

"The doctor said the baby is fairly small but healthy, Irish. He thinks you'll make it through without a cesarean delivery," Max stated quietly. "I don't want anything to happen to either one of you."

"Nothing is going to happen, Max. You'll be there, remember?"

Max looked at her, his dark eyes flickering. "Such trust. What if I come apart? What if I faint?"

She ran a finger down the groove next to his mouth. "Then MacMannis will toss you over her shoulder and carry you off."

Max caught the finger in his mouth, nibbling it. "Did I ever tell you how much those exercises you do turn me on?"

"Nah. No way."

"Wanna bet?" Max murmured, drawing her into his arms.

* * *

In the kitchen, Max retained his image of a swashbuckler boarding a new prize ship.

"Back off, Max," Irish ordered as Max checked his grocery list. "We are not having truffled capon for Thanksgiving. We're having turkey, turkey, turkey. Plain old turkey buffet with pumpkin pie and whipped cream. With mashed potatoes and green beans. With apple pie and Waldorf salad. Plain stuff the guests count on year after year."

Living with Max wasn't easy, she decided, watching him digest the thought of "plain stuff." On Max's "Wednesday Night" she allowed him to cook to his heart's delight. The guests picked suspiciously at the food while Max hovered with the perfect wine to compliment the dish. His selection of dinner music drove most of them to the local tavern where they could dance to country tunes, drink draft beer and eat stale pretzels.

He arched his left brow, the disbelieving one. Then he leveled a contemplative look at her. "Turkey—with oyster stuffing?"

Irish leaned against the counter and placed her fist on her waist—what she could find of it. "With giblets," she said tightly, rubbing her lower back.

Max's hand found the matching spot in his spine. "What about truffled turkey? Or I could..." Max sifted through an immense collection of recipes, all of them untried. Jabbing his finger on a prize, he said, "There. You couldn't ask for anything better than a ham in decorated crust."

Riffling through the recipes, he snatched another treasure. "*Pintades au champagne*—stuffed guinea hens. The guests will love them...." He stopped in midsentence, his eyes flickering as he rubbed his back and stretched painfully. "Damn! My back is getting ready to go out. Aches. Old soccer injury."

Irish rubbed her lower back and scowled at him. "Max, you know what's happening, don't you?"

He scowled back, rubbing the injury. "Yes, damnit, I do. You're not receptive to new foods. I want stuffed capons for Thanksgiving."

She stared at him and took a deep steadying breath. "I refuse to argue the point. Abagail's is having turkey and pumpkin pie made from fresh field pumpkins. The tom is stuffed with natural grains and all dolled up. You put anything else on my table and I won't be responsible for the guests. You may be invited to a tar-and-feather party." Just then Irish had a magnificent stroke of genius. There were more subtle ways to pay Max back for invading her kingdom, for wrapping her in cotton wool so tightly she couldn't move without him at her side.

That evening, Max knelt beside Irish in the dimly lit room of the hospital. According to him, the peaceful background music lacked technique but was just Mac-Mannis's style.

He held Irish's hand and counted her slow deep chest breaths; she found his soft male chanting almost seductive. Max would look delectable in hospital scrubs, Irish thought while he coached her calmly à la MacMannis. "The contraction is ending...take a deep cleansing breath. In through your nose, now let it out...slowly...let it all out."

Concentrating on his wristwatch, Max frowned and glanced down at her. "Breathe, Irish. This is not game time, you know. We're not having the turkey-versus-capon debate now. MacMannis said sixty-second contractions— that's the deal. If we can pass these, we'll move on to the fast chest breathing. Remember, you take deep cleansing breaths before the contraction starts and when you feel it leaving..."

She looked up at him, straightening her red cotton knit maternity top over the baby who tried to kick it off. "Max, are you sure you want to interfere with Abagail's traditional turkey buffet?" she asked carefully while Max checked his watch to prepare for a new sixty-second contraction.

"There are some things a man just has to do," he muttered, getting the go-for-the-gusto look on his face. "Now you remember the uterine stroking, don't you? Get ready..."

Irish thought about her plan through the fast shallow "hee... hee..." breaths at the peak of her sixty-second contraction. The slide into the second stage of labor, "transition," had totally absorbed Max.

"Turkey," she said after the last cleansing breath.

"Capon. Shh. MacMannis is talking about dilating and centimeters. All this information is really going to be helpful. Everything is going to be systematic, running on a schedule. A piece of cake. The monitors will track the baby's heartbeat and your contractions. A surgical crew will be standing by... but you won't need them... there's nothing to worry about." Max adjusted the pillow under her back and rubbed her tummy absently as though she were Mimi. "Dr. Williams asked me to stop by the delivery room after this session. He wants The Whiz to check out some transportation stocks...."

Practicing controlled breathing while driving home wasn't easy for Irish. If Max wanted to play hardball on her side of the street, or bake capons in her oven, he'd have to be able to stand the heat. She had Max's payback waiting at the local tavern, Big Jakes.

Of course Max would stop at Big Jakes. He was always very understanding and patient about her frequent visits to the washroom.

In front of the tavern's neon sign, Max buttoned her coat and tucked her collar high around her throat before he let her out of the station wagon. Irish kissed him, almost feeling guilty that they had now arrived at the scene of her intended crime. Patting his cheek, she smiled. "This won't take a minute."

Big Jakes was a classic tavern. The stereotyped dress code was cowboys in pearl-buttoned shirts, jeans and boots, and women wearing the same. Smoke and cooking grease swirled around the tables. Sad songs about love-gone-wrong drifted over the noise. In a corner, a cowboy's tears dripped into his mug of beer.

Max sheltered Irish with his body as a burly man wearing a cowboy hat with a band of pheasant feathers staggered by them. Over the entire scene floated a marvelous aroma of "the best dad-gummed chili dogs ever made." Served with chopped onions and cheese, the foot long 'dogs were served on freshly baked buns and accompanied by batter-fried, baked-potato wedges.

After her visit to the ladies' room, Irish caught sight of Max leaning against a wall. Wearing a shearling coat and jeans, he blended with the Westerners.

Easing past a couple two-stepping to a fast country-and-western tune, Irish touched Max's arm just as a loud burp roared toward them. Wrapping his arm around her shoulders protectively, Max started toward the door.

"Oh, Max," she cooed, digging in her heels. "Wouldn't you just love a Big Jakes 'dog?"

His arm insisted gently and Irish grabbed the back of a chair. "I want one, sweetheart," she stated flatly, dragging the chair with her for a few inches.

"A hot dog. I'll make you one at the inn. Let's go."

"But, Max. I'm craving one of these."

Max's patience lasted until she ordered a banana split, pickles and chips. He rubbed his flat stomach, eyeing the food before her.

The trick was not to have the beer, Irish thought, watching him slowly pale.

And while he was watching her, Max had sipped a tall mug of draft beer with an inch of foam.

"I think I have heartburn," he admitted slowly when she crunched on the last pickle.

"Max, I've been intending to talk with you," Irish said, leaning back in her chair and nibbling on her last chip. "You're much too serious—lighten up. Remember that childbirth is going to be a piece of cake. Want to dance?"

Max's heavy brows shot together, his eyes narrowing at her. "Just what are you trying to pull, Van Damme?"

Irish grinned, feeling for once that she had the upper hand. "Daddies need to know they haven't lost their touch, don't they? I mean, just because you're expecting doesn't mean you're totally over the hill and unappealing."

The dark flickering dangerous light in Max's eyes promised her an experience she wouldn't soon forget.

"Dance? Where?" he asked, scowling at a couple laminated to each other and swaying to the beat of the music.

Later, swaying to the beat and placing her cheek on Max's broad chest, Irish was totally happy. Because Max had been such a good sport, she rubbed that aching place low on his back while they danced a slow sensuous two-step. Because Max reacted so wonderfully and did enormous things for her ego, Irish placed her lips against his warm throat and nibbled just the way he liked it.

His long frustrated groan preceded Max's hot sweet kiss. Always proper, Max's response startled her into locking her arms around his neck and returning the kiss. When it was finished, they stared into each other's eyes, breathing hard.

"Must be love," a cowboy said in a whiskey voice beside them. "I heard this guy's too stiff-necked and tough to heat up a dance floor. Sure doesn't look like a block of ice to me."

Max's blush preceded a good-natured sheepish grin as the cowboy clapped him on the back. "Congratulations, Pop. Irish is topnotch hereabouts. If she can kiss you like that, you're okay with us."

Nine

In her last month, Irish surrendered her kitchen to the measuring maniac. She'd completely lost control of Abagail's under Max's fruitcake-and-Christmas-cookie siege.

While managing the ranch with The Whiz backing him up, Max nurtured and hugged Irish. He watched her like a hawk and handled all the little niceties of Christmas. Like strudel and dough baked in the shape of Christmas trees. Like filling the guests' stockings with dainty little cookies and candies.

Irish exercised, rubbed Max's aching lower back and watched her TLC kingdom continue merrily along without her.

The chilled skiers delighted in challenging Max on the slopes. They relished his clove-and-orange-juice grog, chicken-noodle soup with chives, and hot cider with lemon wedges. The Whiz, Link and Nadia played poker with Max until he won all their frosted fudge nutty brownies. Jonathan sent a card he had designed, inviting them to his first rave showing.

Tonight, at Abagail's New Year's Eve party, Max dressed in a cotton ski sweater and jeans. He glowed and threw off sexy laser beams that attracted women of all ages. For Max, Abagail would have gladly taken a deadly bullet in her bosom without regret. Women—unpregnant and lithe— tossed passes at him.

Across the parlor from Irish, Max winked at her. Irish lifted her nose and looked away; she knew he was trying to worm his way into her affections when he'd just served a dish outrageously scampied and truffled. Not down-home seasonal cooking at all. His clam chowder was delicious, she admitted reluctantly. So was his French bread, baked over cornmeal in special pans instead of her cookie sheets.

Seated on a comfortable overstuffed chair with her feet propped up as per Max's instructions, Irish thought of the way Max's kisses had changed in the privacy of their bedroom.

Long sweet kisses, dipped in a tasty dampered hunger and sprinkled with rewarding frustrated male groans.

She rubbed the baby, easing the tightness just under her diaphragm. Max called the baby "Jones" after a cabaret dancer he'd found listed in the madam's memoirs. Nadia had completed her first manuscript, tossed it out to the publishing wolves and had zeroed in on developing a biography of Madame Abagail LaRue Whitehouse. Apparently, Jones, a tiny Frenchwoman, could kick the hat out of a tall cowboy's hand.

Jones, Max said, was also a famous football player who kicked the winning ball in some obscure game. Cabaret or football kicker, Max didn't care.

Irish noted a long lithe brunette with a tiny waist and snaky hips making her way toward Max. Carefully arranging pâtés, canapés and quiches away from the eggnog and cracker-and-cheese trays, Max barely seemed to register the brunette's hot-pink fingernails on his cream-colored sweater. The nails traced his broad shoulder while Max slid the smoked salmon nearer the cheese-ball side.

Irish wanted to waddle over and snatch him from Snake Hips. But instead she practiced her candle-blowing breathing exercise and concentrated on willing one part of her body to relax at a time. She'd been exercising muscles she hadn't known were available, preparing for the birth, and now they started constricting rhythmically.

After all, Max wasn't a brunette's oyster Rockefeller waiting to be plucked from a serving tray. He was happier than a clam in lemon dip. Or was he?

Max glanced at Irish. She was curled in a huge overstuffed chair, looking small and very pregnant in her pink maternity overalls.

His stomach contracted sharply, fear tearing through him. Irish needed to be loved, really loved, by a man who knew all the right things to do. But Irish didn't have a man who knew how to love; she had him, he thought as he walked toward her.

"Hi, beautiful," he said, kneeling at Irish's side.

Misty pansy-blue eyes stared up at him and the single tear coursing down her cheek caught Max broadside. His heart beat painfully in his chest, his throat drying. "What's wrong, Irish?"

She sniffed delicately and another tear slid down her cheek. "You should be skiing in Switzerland. Not stuck with me in the middle of dull Colorado. Max, I want you to start thinking about an annulment. Just because I trapped you doesn't mean you have to spend your life paying for it . . . and . . . you'd have visitation rights, too," she finished on a sob. "We're adults. We could manage. . . ."

"What?" Without thinking, Max scooped Irish up in his arms and carried her upstairs.

After placing her on the bed, Max locked the door. "I don't want any interruptions for this discussion. To set the record straight, I wouldn't be here if I didn't want to be. Got it, pansy-eyes?"

God help me, he thought, watching the tears skimming down her cheeks. Clinging to her silvery-gold eyelashes, each shimmering drop wounded him. *He had to convince her that he cared. That he loved her.*

Instead Max sat on the bed and took her hand. "This isn't a temporary affair, Irish. I thought you knew how I felt."

"I'll never be anything like you need, Max." She sniffed, turning away from him. "Go away. Go play with the brunette with the hot-pink fingernails."

"What?" At a loss, Max shook his head and ran his hands through his hair. "What are you talking about?"

"Sex. Here you are, duty bound to a pumpkin." Irish's muffled voice was ragged, drenched in unsobbed tears.

Max blinked, feeling as though he'd just stepped into a world of fairies and gnomes with no road map. One wrong word could land him in the toadstools-and-snakes section.

He filtered through the right things to say, dismissing most of the list as clichés. What he needed for Irish was new and fresh—a genuine mix of words that had never crossed another lover's lips. "I'm married to a sexy pink pumpkin whom—"

Irish's frustrated wail squashed his brief glimpse of success. "See? *A pumpkin!* You feel obligated to cater to me, but you really think I'm a pumpkin. Go pat Mimi. Go rub Morticia's ears."

Whom I love, he'd been about to say. Mimi and Morticia were pushovers. In comparison, Irish was a hard-nosed brute.

And she held the key to his heart, his future.

Downstairs someone started playing an old Sonny and Cher tune to bongo drums, and Max found the erratic rhythm matching his heartbeat. If romantic whimsy was what Irish needed to convince her of his affections—his love—she'd have it. Max rubbed the back of his neck, foraging for just the right words.

After carefully removing Irish's sneakers, he removed his loafers and lay down beside her. He nudged the pillow's pink ruffle aside and studied the antique chandelier overhead. Relating to an emotional pregnant wife wasn't all that easy, he decided as Irish kept her stiff back firmly turned away from him. The nuances of a bordello madam clung to the room; in the past century a cowboy had managed to sway Abagail with romance. Max frowned, concentrating on the brass cupids hanging from the chandelier and trying to draw from these nuances, which Nadia vowed inhabited the room. He tried to tap into that long-ago lover's sweet talk.

The cupids grinned contemptuously down at him.

Irish sniffed again and Max shuddered. Logic wasn't the answer, and whimsy wasn't his style. He'd told her with his body, but now she needed more....

Max ran his fingers through his hair. Telling a woman you love her shouldn't be that difficult, he thought. They'd broken the rules when they started, but he wouldn't have Irish pay for his inadequacies.

Then Irish sniffed again and Max found his fingers smoothing the soft mass of her hair. The curls wound around his hand, clinging to him as softly as Irish had captured his heart.

Coyotes yelped on the mountain and the lonely sound penetrated the room, carrying over the howling winter wind. Snowflakes dusted the windows as Max turned Irish carefully to him.

He blotted her lids with the ruffle, kissing away the tears. Holding her, Max stepped cautiously into whimsy, testing the treacherous waters. "Once upon a time," he began, stroking her hair, "a cowboy came riding out of the West. A wild range rider, a hired gun, bent on suiting himself and—"

"Riding a black Arabian stallion with a silver-studded saddle," Irish interrupted between sniffs, her cheek riding his shoulder.

Max blew aside a reddish-gold tendril. "Hmm?"

Irish nuzzled his shoulder, finding a comfortable spot while Max stroked her lower back. "At least make him sexy, Max."

"Ah . . . the wild range rider and hired gun rode a black sexy stallion. Is that better?"

She shrugged, slipping an arm around him as the bongos started throbbing. "Uh-huh. This should be interesting, Max. A change from your lists and orders."

He smiled, placing his chin comfortably on top of her head. "Okay. But there's a moral in here. You just have to let me forage for it."

"Hmph! Go ahead. . . ." Irish rubbed Max's stomach and he closed his eyes. She always seemed to know the best spots to pick.

"The cowboy parked his horse under a tree—so the birds could dive-bomb his expensive polished saddle and sexy black horse with droppings."

Encouraged by her slight giggle, Max continued, "Then, sashaying her rounded hips and bouncing full bosom across the lawn, this blue-eyed vixen with sun-kissed curly locks met the cowboy, stopping him in his tracks—"

"—boots."

"Stopping him in his boots. The cowboy's lecherous hungry eyes drifted down the fair maiden's luscious body, coveting it with evil plans—like counting freckles."

Giggling openly, Irish slipped her hand lower on his stomach and stroked. Max sucked in his breath and fought to continue his tale. "The cowboy had known many women, visited many bordellos in the West. But this bodacious lady offered sweet delights he hadn't yet sampled, and the cowboy needed to indulge . . . refreshing himself in her four-poster bed."

"After disposing of the villain. Practically breaking his nose."

"Ah, yes. Ever after, the cowboy was grateful to the blackguard. You see, the cowboy—"

"The sexy range rider with the big dangerous gun..."

He chuckled at that, leaning down to kiss her lips. Turning her more fully to him, Max kissed her again, enjoying her slow delicious response. Then, smoothing his hand along her hips, Max continued, "Ever after, the range rider never wanted to roam again. The lady had lassoed his hard heart and tamed his restless needs. He fell beneath the spell of her strawberry kisses."

Irish's arms went tightly around his neck and Max gathered her close to him. "Was the cowboy happy forever, Max?" she asked quietly after a moment.

He kissed her damp cheek. "He never knew he could be so happy. Because every day the lady made his life better. To make his life even happier the lady gave him a baby cowboy."

She lifted her head, propping herself up on an elbow while stroking him with her free hand. "Is that really how you feel, Max?"

Max tasted the lusciously soft strawberry lips of the lady, turning her on her back.

Reaching for him, Irish held him tightly and returned the kiss with all her loving heart.

"Oh, Max," she murmured in a distressed tone just as he was working up to telling her he loved her.

"Mmm?"

"Max, my chest..."

He nestled against her, luxuriating in her lush softness. "Oh, Max, I've dampened myself," she whispered shakily, her pansy-blue eyes staring up at him helplessly.

The tiny twin spots darkening the pink cotton top reminded Max of the baby. Of the love he had yet to profess and the doubts that he needed to waylay for Irish. "I think," he said slowly, running the tip of his finger across her full breasts, "that this may be the loveliest, most exciting sight in my life. Your body preparing for my baby. The baby we made together because we cared..."

"Oh, Max," she cried achingly, throwing her arms around him tightly. "You say the sweetest things. Even if you're just trying to make me feel better."

While he held Irish, Max stared at the mocking cupids on the chandelier. Before the baby arrived, he had to convince her that his love would last.

The next morning while Irish was sleeping, Max saddled a powerful black stallion, Guy de Charlemagne. The horse matched the sexy-stallion description in the range-rider story. Tugging up his shearling coat against the biting Arctic wind, Max nudged Guy's side with his boots. The horse responded in a powerful surge of muscles under a sleek coat, picking his way through the snow-covered peony fields and the zigzagging rows of dead cornstalks.

In the snow and the pines, Max prepared himself for what he must do. *His only chance rested in the thing he least wanted to do—invite his parents to the inn, exposing himself again to their cold hearts. Exposing his wife and child. Yet it would please Irish. And just maybe...*

He shivered and huddled beneath the warmth of the shearling coat, the yawning white abyss in front of him no colder than his past.

Max drew the brim of his Stetson lower, protection against the biting winds. *For Irish's love, he'd walk through hell or into his past.*

Irish looked in the mirror, hating her freckles and heavy jumble of curls. The navy jumper and cornflower-blue frilly blouse didn't hide Plain Old Irish. She looked like a pregnant Raggedy Ann doll. In half an hour the Van Dammes were arriving to meet their daughter-in-law and mother of their coming grandchild.

Since inviting them to Abagail's, Max had suddenly lost his devastating sexy smile. The naughty-boy twinkle was gone.

Tucking a wayward curl behind her ear with Abagail's tortoiseshell comb, Irish smiled brightly into the madam's boudoir mirror. "This is all going to turn out just peachy," she told her reflection. "Max didn't want to do this—but he did. He did it for me, and everything is going to be fine. Jones has a right to know his grandparents on both sides."

She patted the baby who kicked back at her. "Isn't everything peachy in there?" she asked. When Jones kicked again, Irish grinned. "There. Let's go find your father. He's in a snit and playing with his gizmos because he's frightened. We'll protect him, won't we?"

Holed up with The Whiz, Max propped his boots on a desk, and leaned back on the chair's hind legs. Looking lean and cowboylike in his flannel shirt and jeans, Max had never been so appealing.

When he looked at her, his eyes lit up and his hard expression slid away with the sounds of Granny's computer printer. He held out his hand and Irish took it, sliding onto his lap.

"Jones and I had a talk, Max. He's worried about you," she said, smoothing the taut muscle at the back of Max's neck.

Granny muttered that pork bellies had dropped in the stock market, grabbed the computer printout and ran to ask Nadia's opinion of the future stock picture.

Irish leaned her forehead against his. "Max, why don't you whip up something gooey and sinful while we're waiting for your parents?"

His eyebrows went up and the hand caressing her stomach stopped. "Are you feeling all right? The last I remembered we were having a battle over whether pecans were legal in fruitcake. I only agreed to walnuts because you said Jones wanted them."

Irish fluttered her lashes, prying a grin from him despite his tense mood. "Please, Maxi?"

When he chuckled, easing her to her feet, Irish knew that the Van Dammes would be pushovers. Because he walked through perilous times, Irish framed his rugged face with her palms and urged him down for the sweetest kiss her heart could manage.

When the kiss ended, Max hauled her close and stood holding her for a long time.

His parents arrived promptly, taking a taxi from the nearest airport.

Max, dressed in a maroon ski sweater and jeans, greeted them at the front porch. At his side, Irish held his hand and swallowed the last of his honey-coated walnuts.

Elena Van Damme was tall and rawboned. Her eyes were the same shade as Max's; they penetrated as they touched Irish, flowed down the navy jumper and blouse, measuring and predicting everything about the baby. After being seated in the parlor, Elena's movements were efficient, her hands carefully folded on her lap. She looked as though she could remain in the same position forever.

With stooped shoulders, Franz sat carefully beside his wife's stately erect body. Though graying, his hair was the same auburn shade as Max's. When he talked about his latest research, his eyes lit up behind his glasses and his hands were beautifully expressive.

Seated at Irish's side, Max held her hand on his hard thigh. He talked quietly, responding to his father with the same reserve he'd shown when first meeting her. Only his fingers and the hard muscle beneath their hands showed the strain.

Isolated from the scientific discussion that Franz began immediately, Irish studied the Van Dammes. Their relationship was tense; Franz shifted restlessly as he glanced at Elena. The only movement the elder Mrs. Van Damme made for half an hour was to pat her husband's hand just once. Irish and Max shared a long stare of understanding, and then Max inhaled sharply, holding his breath. His hand tightened on hers and, without hesitation, Irish reached up to kiss his cheek.

Immediately his expression changed, his dark eyes lighting as he looked into hers. Abagail's tortoiseshell comb began to slip, and before she could replace it, Max had carefully tucked it back into her curls. His fingers lingered, testing a soft strand. When she began to smile up at him, Max briefly kissed her mouth.

Franz shifted uncomfortably. "Ah, Max. Elena and I thought a fully researched genetic chart for all the families involved might be in order."

Instantly Max turned toward his father, his face hard. "No...thank you," he said with the force of a slammed door.

Elena's head went back slightly, and Franz swallowed with apparent effort. A muscle contracted in Max's cheek; the tension crackled around the room.

In that second Irish ached for Max and his parents. The distance was years deep and would stretch into the future if not stopped. Max needed her help, and from their anxious expressions, so did his parents.

"I think a genetic chart for the baby would be lovely," Irish said, patting Franz's hand as she stood. "My family would just love to help out. Elena, would you like to help me in the kitchen? Max has made some cakes—we can have them with our tea."

Leaning down, she whispered in Max's ear, "You are to show him your computer setup, explain the gizmos and return back here in exactly half an hour. Got it, Maxi?"

When he looked like he might rebel, Irish kissed his hard mouth and treated his parents to Max's naughty-boy look. She flashed the astonished Van Dammes a wide smile and found Elena warily returning it after a moment.

In the kitchen, Elena stood aside while Irish prepared the tea tray. His mother toyed with Max's petits fours, rearranging them on the tray into exact rows. "Max made these?" Elena asked carefully, tracing the delicate pink frosted flowers decorating the tiny cakes.

When Irish nodded, sensing that the older woman wanted to talk, Elena said slowly, "They're lovely. He was such a beautiful little boy."

The wistful aching tone caught Irish and she took Elena's larger hand. "Max is a beautiful man."

Elena's eyes darkened with emotion; her fingers clung to Irish's. "Is he truly happy at last? How I've wondered about him. We haven't been close, you see."

The personal admission had cost Elena, her eyes bright with unshed tears. "Franz and I were too engrossed in our careers when Max came along."

She looked away from Irish, her voice raw with emotion. "We regret our mistake. He was just a baby, and then suddenly he was a young man. He was loved, but I'm afraid that Franz and I aren't very demonstrative...."

Without a second thought, Irish reached up to kiss the older woman's cheek. "The wonderful thing about the past is that it is past—the future and your grandchild is waiting for us. The baby and I will need you to protect us from Max. He can be such a tyrant."

Slowly Elena turned to Irish, smiling softly. "He does make lovely escargot.... Then we're welcome to visit again?"

Irish hugged her, and after an initial stiffening, Elena carefully returned the embrace. "Franz will be elated," she said formally, but her dark eyes were shining.

When his parents left for their home in Missouri, Max turned to Irish. "Wonderful, aren't they?" he asked coldly.

She kissed his cheek and hugged him close—as close as the baby would allow. She definitely had plans to narrow the gap between the Van Dammes, but right now Max needed cuddling. "*You're* wonderful. And now you're mine, not theirs."

Max's naughty-boy twinkle sprang back into his eyes. "You mean you're not offering me an annulment?"

Tracing the firm line of his mouth, Irish leaned back in his arms. "Of course not. Without me, they might never know their grandchild. Without their grandchildren, they might never know love."

She kissed him, slowly, carefully. "Thank you, Max. Meeting the grandparents of our baby meant very much to me. And I know how difficult it was for you to see them under the circumstances."

Max shuddered, gathering her closer. "You have no idea."

"Poor Max. Poor Daddy," she said, meaning it and cuddling nearer to him. "He's going to be fine. We'll have fantastic family reunions with Pop teaching Franz and Jones how to play football. Mother and Elena can fish in the creek while you and I—"

Max's hard kiss stopped her from finishing.

By the last of January the baby had lowered into birthing position, allowing Irish to breathe easier.

Max seemed to be constantly tired, tense and anxious while Irish felt great. She began freestyle cooking again and helped Nadia with the last stages of her manuscript. Plotting her successful future on tarot cards and confident of a sale, Nadia sailed off to New York.

The first week of February swept into the valley on an unexpected blizzard. The fierce storm stranded Granny and Link in Denver. Maudie Kleinhauser had been offended by Nat Johnson, who said women couldn't manage without men and had rallied the support of Kodiac's "womenfolk." Lizzie Caulder's husband didn't act as romantic as Max, and she added to the mutiny by ordering that all the children be left in charge of the "menfolk." The hostile women had barricaded themselves in a neighboring town's high-school gym and were having a glorious time despite the weather.

Alone with Max, Irish watched the snow fall softly across the fields. The weather prediction was for several inches; the mountain passes were already blocked by heavier snow. The storm hovered over the valley all day, and on the second morning, Irish padded around the kitchen, making Max's favorite pancakes—lumberjack buttermilk pancakes with tiny bits of apple in them.

With just the two of them, Irish had chosen to use the old wood cookstove. The electricity had been chancy since early dawn, and cozy warmth added to Irish's happy mood. While Max was busy with the outside chores, she arranged the spices her way.

Jones hadn't kicked all night, and Irish felt as if she could clean Abagail's from top to bottom by herself. Because she felt so wonderful, Irish had showered and dressed in Max's favorite blue frilly nightgown. The granny-styled garment never failed to rate a magnificent, ego-building, first-class seductive kiss.

Max had developed a sexy Western look that could take her breath away at ten paces; he looked like Abagail's handsome cowboy lover. Alone with him, she discovered that he liked nothing better than watching old movies while eating popcorn.

She plopped a spoonful of batter onto the griddle and grinned. She'd introduced Max to a marvelous game of drive-in movie. It had to do with snuggling on the couch, and Max, though careful of the baby, delighted in playing sensual games with her. He said he didn't mind the cold showers and he'd started lifting car bumpers for a hobby.

He didn't appear to feel trapped by impending fatherhood.

Bringing in the wood for the day, Max tromped the excess snow from his boots on the back porch and entered the kitchen in a flurry of snowflakes.

He placed the wood in the box, dusted his leather gloves and tucked them in his pocket. Shrugging off his coat, he leaned down to kiss her, his face cold and ruggedly appealing. "Dear heart," he murmured in the raspy steamy voice that warmed her as his eyes took in the gown.

Setting out to earn the nickname, Irish put her heart into the long slow kiss.

"Oh, Max!" she exclaimed a moment later when warm water trickled down her legs.

He looked at the puddle forming at her feet, frowned and yanked a towel from the rack. Lifting her gown, Max tucked the towel between her legs and carried her to a chair. "First stage of labor. The baby is coming," he announced grimly, picking up the telephone receiver.

Max's face darkened, his eyebrows drawing together in a single line and his lips pressed together as he listened. "Lines are out."

He frowned at her, then down at Jones. "Are you having contractions?"

Irish's eyes widened as she realized that all morning she'd been getting warning signs. There was just that slight tightening across her stomach and... "My back hurts," she said quietly, watching the fear leap in his eyes.

"We're here alone, Irish," Max stated, moving toward her, his expression grim. "There isn't a chance of anyone coming in or us making it to the hospital."

He shivered and Irish placed her palm on his cheek. "Don't worry, Max."

Gripping her hand and bringing it to his mouth, Max frowned. "Irish, I'm going downstairs to switch on the electric generator and then I'm coming back."

The pancakes began to burn. "Max, the pancakes—"

"Pancakes, hell," he muttered, flipping them expertly and placing the griddle aside. Checking the antique stove's water reservoir and finding it filled, Max ran down the basement stairs.

In a matter of seconds the generator thudded comfortably below them.

"Oh, Max," Irish managed as he ran back up the stairs and scooped her up in his arms.

Carrying her to the couch, Max placed pillows behind her back and stripped her briefs from her gently. His hands moved on her carefully, tracing the baby's arrival.

Wiping his hand across his brow, Max took her hand. "Lady, you and I are in love," he stated roughly. "I've been wanting to say it in pretty ways, ways to make it new and special to you. But now the baby isn't waiting for anything, and I want you to know you are my life and more to me. There isn't going to be an annulment and we're going to raise our baby together. I love you. Got it?"

She inhaled, fighting the urge to cry. "What a time..." When Max's face paled, she gripped his hand. He needed everything she could give him and she gave him her love. "Got it."

Gathering her to him, he kissed her hard. "You've got to trust me now, Irish."

"Max...don't debate the point...I love you," she said as his hands moved over her, seeking the baby.

He frowned, arranging the towel beneath her. Taking a deep breath, Max attempted a carefree grin. The one that could make her melt—at other times. "Actually, I've talked to MacMannis and Dr. Williams about a home delivery, and they made me a list. Dr. Williams gave me his favorite stethoscope—a thank-you for connecting him to The Whiz who's been busy researching library banks. He's been hoping that he could fly down in the helicopter, and now he's going to get his wish. While he's taking care of you, I'm going to stuff him with German and French dishes."

She caressed his cheek, loving him. "Always prepared, Max."

When he grinned sheepishly and kissed her hand, Irish grinned back. "Get your notebook, Max."

"Well," he said, standing slowly, "this is where the sturdy foldaway bed and the portable radio system to MacMannis is important. I designed a special beeper for her and it will only take a minute to set up—she'll talk us through this. Then with the generator working we can use the home contraction monitor.... "

"Hurry, Max," Irish gritted between her teeth as another contraction hit her.

He placed his hand over the baby, read his watch, timing the contraction while he coached her breathing. After her cleansing breath, Max swung into action.

Two hours later the snow kept falling outside and the pains began coming closer together. Lying on clean sheets on a comfortable cot in the warm kitchen, Irish watched Max talk quietly to MacMannis. "Three minutes apart and lasting forty-five seconds—yes, of course I measured. She's up to eight centimeters—yes, I know it's coming fast, damn it."

"Max, be nice," Irish urged softly, listening to Max storm quietly at the nurse.

"She's in transition, dammit," he snarled impatiently, glancing at Irish who had just begun to feel another sharp contraction. "Yes, I know they get nasty and I'm prepared—"

"Max, dammit, get your buns over here," Irish snapped.

His eyes widened momentarily as though she'd just slapped him. Irish began breathing desperately, feeling as though she'd *like* to slap him. "Max, get your lists and get the hell over here," she managed, breathing heavily. "Or the deal is off."

While he stared blankly at her, Irish glared at him. "That does it," she muttered, struggling to rise from the cot. "I've changed my mind. I'm going upstairs and forgetting about you forever. You pop in here loaded for bear..."

"Irish," Max finally said, moving swiftly toward her. "Honey, lie down—"

"Yes, I did lie down—with you. Hell's bells, now I know what can happen when a range rider shows up at my doorstep," she managed as another contraction zigzagged through her.

Max held her hand and coached her through the painful interval. When it was finished, Irish was sweaty, lying back to doze momentarily.

Max's hands moved over her, his paper lists shuffling in the notebook. Adjusting the speaker to his head, he spoke quietly to MacMannis. "She's nasty-tempered. Yes, I know the snow has stopped...where is the helicopter now...okay, yes...easy, Irish...MacMannis says you deserve a medal for putting up with me...."

Rolling Irish gently to her left side, Max used the base of his palm to rub her back. "You're doing great, sweetheart. That's right, take a rest. Remember on our next contraction, we're breathing hee-hee-hee, who-who-who-ing...."

Irish glared at him. "What do you mean, *our* next contraction?" she managed just as the pain began. Max talked calmly into the mouthpiece, flipping his manual with one hand and holding her hand with the other.

"Yes, Irish is beautiful...yes, dammit, I love my wife...no, I haven't told her enough.... Irish, I love you," Max stated flatly. "I love you. See, MacMannis, I told her...the storm's over...he'd better get here fast...now, shut up...of course I won't stop saying it when the baby is born...yes, I see your note about crowning in paragraph five...."

Irish began working hard, concentrating on breathing, concentrating on her love for Max, and resting. When the contractions began again she pushed, squeezing Max's big secure hand and obeying his commands.

Max loved her; the lines on his face deepened with concern, his kisses punctuating the easier moments. After a heavy contraction, he attempted a lopsided beguiling smile. "Still want to change your mind and go upstairs, sweetheart?"

"Tell me you love me. Now," she demanded when he wiped her forehead with a cool cloth. "And what happened to 'dear heart'?"

Max's hands stopped moving over her. "You are the sunshine of my heart. You took me from the cold and made me yours," he said in a deep tone of raw emotion, tears coming to his eyes.

Another pain peaked and Irish pushed against his hands. "You can do this, Max.... Hell's bells," she gasped. "You can love this baby. You'll give him every drop of love he needs...."

Irish closed her eyes, working with the contraction. In the distance, a door opened and closed and a burst of Arctic air entered the room.

When she opened her eyes, Dr. Williams stood near Max, drawing on his gloves. He held them up for Irish to see. "Baby time," he said cheerfully, stepping briskly into position. "You owe me some fancy cooking for that helicopter ride. But right now, give Mama something to push against and let's get that baby here in time for supper."

"Dear heart..." Max began, leaning over her.

"That's it, talk to her. Irish, let's go. We can do this in just a few minutes. We're practically home free...."

"Ah, Max," Dr. Williams said a few moments later. "You've done a fine job, followed my orders perfectly. Now how about holding your daughter?"

Irish had a glimpse of Max's astonished expression, the tearful joy filling it before he handed the tiny squirming baby to her.

Max wiped away a tear running down his cheek, then dabbed Irish's tear trails. "She's beautiful," he managed raggedly as the baby nuzzled at Irish, seeking nourishment. "Perfectly beautiful," he repeated in an awed tone.

Dr. Williams's firm order cut through the moment. "Max, you're woozy. If you're going to pass out, sit down. Now."

For once, Max obeyed and poured his tall body into a kitchen chair.

Irish's love for him rose, trembled on the afternoon air and filled the room. Looking helpless and vulnerable, Max continued to stare blankly at her and the baby. "Daddy, we love you," she called gently.

He grinned slowly, sheepishly, responding to her. "Say hi to Daddy, baby," Irish whispered to her daughter nestling against her breast.

When she waved the baby's tiny hand at Max, he waved back, grinning widely. "Hi, Jones."

"I'll want lasagna tonight," Dr. Williams said, taking the baby.

Ten

"**B**oonie's hot fudge cake is classless," Max stated flatly. He dropped walnut halves onto the cake's thick layer of chocolate frosting with an air of disdain. The halves hit the frosting to the beat of Beethoven's Fifth Symphony, Max's after-dinner music, which played through the kitchen's sound system.

"See Daddy grumble, Abagail," Irish teased as she held four-month-old Abagail against her shoulder for a last burp. She rubbed the baby's back and kissed the small head covered with a cap of black curls.

Max turned to her, his frown sliding into a warm delighted grin. "Abagail, Daddy's happy to bake Boonie's favorite chocolate cake. Boonie deserves it. See Daddy smile?"

Abagail Serene Van Damme accommodated her parents with a loud but feminine burp. Her head bobbed toward Max and she cooed, blinking pansy-blue eyes.

Standing in his stocking feet, wearing a T-shirt and jeans, Max looked as delicious as the gooey double-chocolate nut cake he'd just created. His auburn hair had caught the early evening June breeze, and the mussed waves caused him to have that living-on-the-edge dangerous-cowboy look that always excited Irish. Abagail LaRue Whitehouse's sequined and lusty heart would have quivered at the sight of Max's cowboy image.

With laughter lines radiating from his dark exciting eyes and his skin weathered by the Colorado sun and wind to a texture that tempted her fingertips and lips to explore, Max was the perfect daddy candidate.

Irish had definite plans to explore Max's lean and accommodating body later in the evening. The Whiz owed Max a debt, and payback involved baby-sitting for a whole night and the next day. Irish had plans that involved slow two-stepping at Big Jakes and... She could almost feel her fingers rummaging through the tuft of hair escaping the neckline of Max's T-shirt.

Abagail Van Damme blew slobbery bubbles at her father and blinked her wide eyes again. "Daddy's little girl won't like gooey fudgey cake, will she? Say 'Abagail wants crepes, Abagail loves crepes,'" Max cooed, his deep raspy voice causing Irish's breasts to peak.

Motherhood had pounced on Irish's breasts as though making a proud announcement to the world. Though the rest of her body had trimmed, her breasts retained a lush contour. This instigated Max's fascination with the precise construction of bras, ballast and support, and caused The Whiz to invest in a special line of lingerie.

Boonie's short rap on the back door signaled his arrival, and Max let him in. Shaking the rancher's hand in genuine warmth, Max said, "Your weekly cake is ready. How are you doing?"

"Doing fine. Been seeing Dortha, but she can't cook. Sure appreciate this cake, Max. I'll have the campsite set up

when you and Irish are done at Big Jakes. Don't forget
that will cost you two cakes for three weeks."

Boonie walked toward Irish, totally ignoring her in pur
suit of Abagail who reached out a tiny hand. "How'
Boonie's peachy-pie little sweetums?" he asked, taking th
hand and kissing it gallantly while Abagail blinked an
blew bubbles at him.

Then he noticed Irish and grinned shyly. "You okay, li
tle mama?" When she returned his grin and nodded
Boonie said, "Got plans for my own family if everythin
works out right. But since I figure Max owes me, I'll still b
coming in for my cake, okay?"

"You're welcome any time, Boonie," she returned
"Even for Max's Wednesday Night dinner."

Boonie shuddered and released Abagail's hand. H
backed toward the door, holding his precious cake a
though fearing Max would retrieve it. "Yuk. The Frenc
snails and smothered-tongue delight," he muttered befor
slipping out the door.

"There is nothing wrong with my escargots," Max mut
tered while drying the kitchen counter. With his nose defi
nitely out of joint, he padded into the laundry room an
returned with an overflowing basket of clean diapers. Sit
ting down at the table, he grumbled about low-class no
taste cowboys while he methodically folded Abagail's dia
pers.

Precisely stacked, the mound of fluffy diapers grew
quickly. When he moved on to the bibs, gowns and jam
mies, Irish handed Abagail to him. She'd found that con
tact with Abagail sweetened Max's rough edges instantly.

Max cuddled the baby to him, his large hand supportin
her bottom while he grinned and toyed with her tiny hands
The baby cooed and waved her fists around, and Ma
chuckled, lifting her for a kiss. She blinked her eyes at hir
and he held her close, rocking her slightly and humming
movement from Bach.

Irish finished the laundry and glanced at him. "Abagail can't come camping, Max. Don't give her any big ideas."

"Definitely not this time, Abagail," he agreed, tossing a wicked grin at Irish. Max cradled Abagail on his thighs and deftly unsnapped her jammies. In less than fifteen seconds he had replaced her diaper, exactly matching the angles of the diaper pins. He snapped the jammies and held Abagail aloft, playing with her.

Watching Max loving Abagail with such delight and pride, Irish caressed his shoulder. "Happy?"

Max's dark eyes swung to hers as he cradled the baby against his chest. "Dear heart, I didn't know there was love until you filled my life," he stated simply in the rough tone she'd come to know as deep emotion.

For that instant, their eyes met and held. Love coursed through the moment like a heavy sweet rhapsody, timeless and strong.

Max's expression when he rocked Abagail was one of absolute peace, of contentment and love. He no longer doubted his ability to love; it radiated from him, spilling into every touch, every quiet sharing moment.

Each night when he at last took Irish in his arms, it was with reverence and love.

Abagail interrupted the long meaningful look when she investigated Max's ear, her cheek gently bumping his, and Max sent Irish a hot promising look that she answered with her own.

"Our first night out," he murmured, lifting her palm. His tongue flicked the sensitive center. "I've got big plans for our date. After Big Jakes—when we're camping."

Irish traced his lips, grinning impishly. "Be careful. I've got some ideas of my own."

Later at Big Jakes, Max surveyed the smoky interior with the air of a range rider scouting for a lookout post. "Our first night out," he said between his teeth, "and you pick a place that smothers chili dogs in fried white onions.

There's a place in Denver that knows how to parboil shal lots with white sauce—''

''Maxi,'' Irish cooed, fluttering her eyelashes at him. She loved how he always stared at her for a moment blankly, as though all the click-click circuits had stopped momentar ily.

Max took a deep unsteady breath, his eyes flowing ap preciatively over the frilly eyelet blouse Irish had chosen for the occasion. The blue lacy-skirt-and-blouse concoction deserved a man who appreciated a woman—one with masses of curly blond hair. ''I can manage,'' he mur mured huskily.

Irish fluttered her eyelashes again. ''I know.''

Because everyone at Big Jakes knew it was the Van Dammes' first after-the-baby night out, Max and Irish re ceived special treatment. Big Jake ladled more chili onto Max's hot dog, but slyly avoided the onions. Mineral wa ter with lime filled their beer mugs and later a bottle of Max's favorite wine appeared at the table—with pretzels.

The Western band played two-step songs, and a cowboy stepped up to the microphone, wailing about his dying love and dying dog. Snuggled against Max's broad chest, Irish managed to find that tempting spot at his throat. When she kissed his warm skin, Max's hands wandered in the dark shadows of a favorite corner.

''We'll have to bring your parents here,'' she whispered against the spot, and Max's hands stopped wandering.

Against her ear, he whispered loudly over the bass gui tar, ''Irish, you've been pushing your luck about my par ents. Sending them Abagail's picture was your idea, and now they want growth charts.''

Irish's nose nuzzled the hair on Max's chest. Having her own range rider, dressed in a Western shirt, was definitely a perk for marriage. She slid her hands into his jeans back pockets to more fully appreciate the taut lean muscle mov ing beneath the denim. ''We can never be one big happy

amily, Irish," Max managed huskily, his hands moving
ower on her lips.

"Well…they are going to visit in the fall. Mom and Pop
.ave agreed to come and run interference if they pick on
'ou. But according to Nadia's readings, they'll enjoy their
.randdaughter so much that you won't have any prob-
ems."

She looked up into Max's dark flickering gaze. "Max,
.ave you ever realized that your parents are the only peo-
.le we know who truly appreciate your escargot recipes?"

He stopped swaying to the music. "You know, I think
hey do appreciate fine cooking."

"And fine wine. When I told them about Van Damme-
)alton vineyards and wine, they decided to research the
.enetic composition of the strain of grapes. Your mother
.sked about the soil composition and breeding for
aste—" She stopped when Max's lips covered hers.

Max fitted her against his body as he had fitted her into
.is life, systematically and devotedly. With gusto supreme
.hat Irish returned in kind.

Big Jake's ham-size hand shook Max's shoulder, inter-
upting the kiss. "Irish, the band wants to try out their first
.ock-and-roll session and need some dancers on the floor.
.ow 'bout it?"

Still wrapped in Max's arm's, Irish gazed up at her hus-
.and, who looked as though he'd like to carry her out into
.he midnight air and kidnap her in his station wagon. Then
.e grinned slowly, devastatingly. "Clear the floor. I won a
.ock-and-roll trophy a few years back."

Irish stared up at him. "You?"

He led her on to the dance floor with the air of a knight
.scorting his lady to the cotillion. While the band warmed
.p, the lead guitar tossing out Chuck Berry segments, Irish
.ossed Max a challenge. "I'm very good, Max," she said,
.onfident he would return the tease.

He lifted an eyebrow, his eyes daring. "Think you're hot
tuff, do you?"

"Tops."

The band started playing, and Max took her hands. The began dancing carefully, following the hard beat an gauging each other's style. Tucking her against him, Ma said, "Dear heart, you ain't seen nothin' yet."

"Take it slow, Pops," she returned just before Ma flipped her across his back.

"Oh, my," she said, just before he picked her up at th waist and Irish found herself sitting briefly on his har thigh. "Oh, my," she repeated when she slid through Max' long legs to emerge on the other side.

"Having fun, Mrs. Van Damme?" he asked as Iris stepped into the beat, and Max twirled her under his arm

"Definitely, Mr. Van Damme," she managed betwee laughing. "Do you think you could squeeze some rock-and roll tapes into the sound system—between Bach an Tchaikovsky?"

"Abagail needs soothing music now. But we could hav it piped into our bedroom when we add those privat apartments to Abagail's Inn."

When they danced later to a slow song, Irish snuggle safely against Max. "Thanks for sneaking those free cou pons to the Hendrichs, Max."

"I don't know anything about it.... Okay, they neede to get away from their problems for a few days," he mu mured against a curling wisp of her hair. "Ah, are we goin to dance all night?"

Located miles from Kodiac, the campsite was in mountainside clearing in the sprawling, rugged Rockies. I the starlit night, the Colorado moon hovered like an ele gant silvery disk.

Boonie had set up a small tent, stocked with cassett player and tapes. Two ice chests were stocked with food and an array of cooking gear waited near a camp fire tha just needed to be lit.

Dominating the clearing was a solid brass four-poster bed covered by a sheet of plastic. Beneath the bed, a large shag carpet covered the pine needles.

Irish watched Max neatly fold and tuck the plastic away, exposing the red satin bedspread. "Nothing like planning," she said as he entered the tent to retrieve the battery-operated cassette player. The strains of Bach immediately flowed through the mountain air.

"Hmm, the old thee-and-me game, huh?" Irish asked when Max finally turned to her. She could feel the heat and the tension growing in the night, sending sweet expectations running along her flesh.

"I wanted tonight to be something you'd remember, dear heart," Max said, his voice deep and raw with emotion. An intense hunger filled his harsh features, the rugged planes and angles catching the moonlight. Max stood several feet away from her, and his tall body was rigid.

They shared the moment silently, thinking of their love. The future would be filled with Abagail and each other, every moment precious.

Then Max began to unbutton his shirt. Following his motions, Irish began loosening her blouse, her eyes holding his.

They undressed slowly, watching the moonlight spill between them, over them, like a silvery magical sheet.

Irish allowed her blouse and skirt to fall at her bare feet. Covering her pale shimmering skin were twin strips of black lace. He followed the curves of her body hungrily, this woman who had brought him love and taken his heart.

She lifted the heavy fall of her hair, the simple gesture reducing him instantly. Max traced the lush new lines of her body: her full pale breasts shimmering in the moonlight above the low-cut bra, and the delicate indentation of her waist flowing into her rounded hips; a thin strip of lace and shadows concealing the joining of her long tapering thighs.

He moved to her swiftly, trimming his passion for the moment and savoring the dark mysterious eyes of his wife.

Tracing her hot cheek with his finger, Max bent his hea and tasted her soft parted mouth.

Her scent filled him with joy; beneath the fresh dais scent, her own seductive musk reached out to ensnare h senses. Irish's soft skin heated to his touch as he knew would, her eyes widening with the emotions trembling o the soft still air. He nibbled her bottom lip, inhaling the sor gasp of pleasure. The movement brought his bare che against her breasts, caressing him.

Skimming her body with the flat of his hands, Ma smoothed her hips, treasuring the softness filling his palm:

Taking his time, Max slipped the lace from her. "Oh Max," she cried out softly as he fitted his mouth over h breast. Lingering on the satiny skin, Max felt her hea pound beneath his lips. Her cries delighted him, heated h passions until he trembled, aching for her.

Max eased his fingers under the lace at her thighs an found the delicate heat waiting for him. Her hand skimmed over him, trembling, touching him intimately wit an awe that always astounded him.

Their lips touched and hovered and fitted together a Max slipped the last shred of lace from her. The delica play of their tongues tempted him to deepen the tantali ing kisses that never satisfied, yet offered more. Still, Ma held back, savoring the fragrance and the gentleness of h wife, his mate, letting her set the pace.

Her palms slid over him as her breasts moved against h hard chest, the twin softness melding gently to him.

He caught her in his arms, lifting her to his chest. "M heart, my love," he whispered against the tumbling mass c her hair.

Irish's arms curved around his neck, her cheek resting o his shoulder. "My love," she echoed softly, stroking h taut chest and soothing the hot immediate hunger momer tarily.

Then Max needed her desperately, and he lowered h gently to the red satin bedspread.

She found him waiting for her, his trembling hands and uneven breath exciting.

The satin moved smoothly at her back, and Max's hard thigh nudged her intimately, his mouth parted and moist on her skin.

His hands ran down her body, claiming, seeking. The fine trembling of his fingers heated her senses immediately, her own hungers stoked and waiting. Tonight while their daughter slept peacefully, they would renew their love and wonder.

Max's hand found her breasts, lingering luxuriously in the moment preceding the passion they would explore. His fingertips traced the sensitive nubs delicately, reverently. His lips followed his touch, tasting her with kisses that made her tremble.

Heating against the long length of Max's hard body, Irish moved swiftly, seeking and finding. She smoothed the rigid contours of corded muscle, tangling her bare thighs with his bulkier ones.

Max shuddered, his hands seeking her softness, his voice rough with passion. She cried out in answering need, her body aching with a poignant sharpness. Moving over Max, Irish fitted their bodies together; they became one, just as their lives had merged.

Poised on the peak of pleasure and passion, Irish stilled, taking into her the wonder of their perfect lives. Max caught the precious timeless moment, held her body in his large safe hands and waited, savoring the very edge of the coming ecstasy.

The fiery peak grew, consuming and flaming on the edge, then drew them down into the heat and urgency of passion. Carefully lowering herself to him, Irish rested for an instant.

Closing her eyes and taking the intense pleasure into her, she ran her palms down his damp hair-roughened chest.

"Dear heart," Max said roughly against her ear, nibbling on the lobe.

While Irish concentrated on his throat, dragging hot kisses along the taut muscular length, Max resorted to drastic tactics and sought her most vulnerable area.

Pressing her hips against him with one hand, Max opened his lips on the spot.

Irish reacted immediately and beautifully. For just a fraction of an instant, Max felt guilty for disturbing her survey of him. Then as she moved swiftly and hungrily against him, the soft cries startling and urgent, Max lost himself in the experience of Irish's passion.

In the moonlight and shadows, she moved over him, binding him to her with love.

He met the delicate savagery of her mouth with hunger, her body flowing over his, taking and yielding.

Her hair caressed his skin, the silky strands binding them as closely as the child they had created.

The pleasure point held as Irish's body closed rhythmically around him, her soft exclamations of pleasure flowing over him, filling him.

He followed her immediately, calling out his love in the fierce driving pleasure.

The night was long and steeped in love, and in the morning, Irish lay snuggled in red satin while Max moved around the camp fire, dressed only in jeans. The morning birds flitted from tree to tree, and chipmunks raced up and down red-barked pines.

A gentle mist hovered in the clearing, and stepping through it, Max served Irish breakfast in bed. He carefully placed the tray across her knees, tugging the red satin bedspread up to her chin. He grinned, looking pleased and very rakish for a systems-warrior husband. "I've noticed that this portion of your anatomy is sensitive to temperature— cold and hot," he explained in the deep raspy tone she loved.

He bent to kiss a tender peak. "When you were pregnant with Abagail, your breasts were delightful."

Then, slipping off his jeans, he joined her in the brass bed. When Irish kissed him, Max lingered in the sweet kiss, tantalizing her. "This must have been Madame Abagail Whitehouse's camping style," she said, nibbling on the spot at the corner of his mouth.

"One learns from the past. According to her diary, the madam used this ploy a few times with her favorite lover," Max stated, nuzzling her throat with his new beard. "Do you like the omelet?"

Irish shared the golden brown mushroom-and-green-pepper mixture with him. "This is marvelous, right down to the daisy bouquet. Max, you are so romantic."

Leaning back against the fluffy satin pillows, Max lounged in all his masculine glory exposing a deeply tanned hair-covered chest. "I try to please," he returned contritely, his hand finding her thigh beneath the satin.

"Maxi, I do love you," Irish murmured, placing aside the tray and curling up to him. She walked her fingers up his chest, fluttering her lashes at him.

A chattering chipmunk ran up a tree, and a bird darted through the hovering mist.

He caught her fingertips, bringing them to his lips. "What's up, pansy-eyes? You've got that look."

Irish fluttered her lashes again, thinking that systems warriors made great husbands. "Hmm? Max, did I ever tell you the story about the fertile Van Dammes? The ones living in Abagail LaRue Whitehouse's bordello? The ones expecting their second baby?"

Max sat up, the red satin sliding downward. He turned her roughly to him, his dark face urgent. "Us?"

"Uh-huh. You do make such a wonderful daddy candidate, darling," Irish murmured before Max kissed her, sweetly and with love.

*　*　*　*　*

Bestselling author NORA ROBERTS captures all the romance, adventure, passion and excitement of Silhouette in a special miniseries.

THE CALHOUN WOMEN

Four charming, beautiful and fiercely independent sisters set out on a search for a missing family heirloom—an emerald necklace—and each finds something even more precious...passionate romance.

Look for THE CALHOUN WOMEN miniseries starting in June.

COURTING CATHERINE
Silhouette Romance #801

July
A MAN FOR AMANDA
Silhouette Desire #649

August
FOR THE LOVE OF LILAH
Silhouette Special Edition #685

September
SUZANNA'S SURRENDER
Silhouette Intimate Moments #397

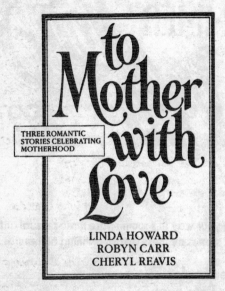
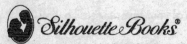